I0679277

Sherlock Holmes and the Affair in Transylvania

Gerry O'Hara

Illustrations by P M Rose

Based upon the Vampire Tales

of Arthur Conan Doyle, Bram Stoker

and J.S. Le Fanu

Paperback: ISBN 9781780920368

ePub: ISBN 9781780920375

PDF: ISBN 9781780920382

Published in the UK by MX Publishing Limited,

335 Princess Park Manor, Royal Drive,

London, N11 3GX.

www.mxpublishing.com

Cover design by www.staunch.com from

illustrations by P M Rose

This book and artwork is dedicated to Kate

CHAPTER ONE

I sometimes wonder if I was ill-advised to disclose, in my recounting of The Problem of Thor Bridge, that in the vaults of my bankers, Messrs Cox & Co., at Charing Cross, there is a travel-worn and battered tin dispatch box with my name, John H. Watson, MD., Late Indian Army, painted upon the lid, crammed with papers, nearly all of which are records of cases to illustrate the curious problems which Mr Sherlock Holmes had at various times to examine. Some, and not the least interesting, were complete failures, and as such will hardly bear narrating, since no final explanation is forthcoming.

Among these unfinished tales is that of Mr James Phillimore, who, stepping back into his own house to get his umbrella, was never more seen in this world.

A second case worthy of note is that of lsadore Persano, the well-known journalist and duellist, who was found stark staring mad with a matchbox in front of him which contained a remarkable worm, said to be unknown to science.

No less remarkable is the case of the cutter, ALICIA, which sailed one spring morning into a small patch of mist from which it never emerged, nor was anything further ever heard of herself and her crew.

It is the strange matter of THE ALICIA which brings to mind the awful, utterly grotesque encounter which I feel solemnly bound to record on these pages, with, of course, the caveat - agreed with my friend and colleague, Sherlock Holmes - that publication shall be withheld until at least fifty years after our demise, whichever shall survive the other.

It is the appalling story of our pursuit of Count Dracula, he of The Undead, Nosferatu. He, too, had the mysterious ability to bring down the mists to cover his heinous activities.

My friend Holmes was apt to describe Professor Moriarty as "The Napoleon of Crime"; of Count Dracula one must say that here was a being so fiendish, so brutally evil as to make Moriarty, arch criminal that he was, of little consequence.

Our involvement began innocently enough. Holmes, at the behest of HMG, had consented to journey to Bucharest to investigate a matter of the utmost delicacy concerning a minor member of the Romanian Royal Family, whose foolishness was causing considerable embarrassment to His Royal Highness King Carol.

As with some of those copious files I have already referred to, the matter is not worthy of report, nor would the airing of such a scandal be appropriate.

His Majesty was deeply grateful for Holmes's incisive handling of the matter and we were both - I as his Boswell, as it were - feted and honoured in the most inappropriate manner. Holmes received The Star and Sash of The Order of St Ignacious and I received the somewhat lesser honour of member of the Order of Istvan The Good. His Majesty graciously invited us to vacation in his beautiful country, offering the use of his hunting lodge in the forest of Bostrut, but my colleague yearned for the real world of 221B, Baker Street and we duly declined.

We elected to take the train to Budapest en route for Calais. His Majesty wished us Godspeed.

Our departure was typical of the extraordinary hospitality of our royal host. A red carpet lay before us as we arrived at the station, accompanied by The King's Ambassador and entourage. A military band, resplendent in gold-piped uniforms, played a most moving rendition of our national anthem. Young women in folk costume overwhelmed us with bouquets of flowers. Holmes did his best not to appear discomfited by all the fuss.

It was moments before departure when a courier, red-faced and breathless, handed Holmes a sheaf of letters and telegrams which had evidently been expressly forwarded to us.

Settled into our reserved compartment for the long journey to Budapest, Holmes went about the business of sorting the mail. Pausing to light his pipe he brusquely produced an envelope addressed to myself. I must say I accepted it with some surprise.

"Good Lord," I remarked, "who on earth could have known I was here?"

Holmes glanced at the envelope again.

"Well now," he murmured, "the envelope is pleasantly scented, the hand-writing is clearly feminine and is surely the product of a good English girls school. It is post-marked Budapest and I do seem to recall that your niece has lately married and settled in that city."

With that he returned to his own correspondence. I tore open the envelope and quickly sought the signature. It was indeed from my delightful young niece, Mina, newly wed and settled in Hungary with her husband, Janos Svbado, an enterprising and lately graduated lawyer.

The opening paragraph of the letter observed the usual obligations of filial courtesies but then descended into a somewhat alarming narrative.

I must have uttered a string of "Oh Lor's" and "I'll be blessed's" because I became aware of an astringent Holmes, pipe in hand, inquiring acidly:

"Just what are you blessed about, may I ask?"

"Two things," I replied. "You were perfectly correct, the letter is from my niece, Mina, though I'm blessed how she knew my whereabouts, Secondly, her husband, young Janos, seems to have disappeared on a journey to Transylvania."

Holmes sighed and pulled on his pipe for a moment.

"The first point," he said, "is hardly surprising, since the Bucharest correspondent of The Times filed regularly on the matter of our visit and, doubtless, the leading journals in other capitals copied his despatches. I expect your niece, homesick as she may be, followed the reports with interest."

I acknowledged the sense of this.

"On the second point," he went on, "I believe Transylvania is situated in a horseshoe of The Carpathians renowned for its wilderness. Indeed I have read that the area is said to have every known superstition in the world gathered there as if it were the centre of some imaginative whirlpool. One must hope that he had not been devoured by wolves."

With that somewhat cynical jest he gave the briefest of smiles and returned to his correspondence.

I continued to concern myself with my niece's letter and certainly intended to get in touch with her when we arrived at Budapest. My friend made no more mention of the matter and I was agreeably surprised when, as the train was drawing in to Vidin, he suggested I should wire Mina to arrange rooms for us as, no doubt, I would wish to offer her comfort in her time of anxiety.

Mina was there to meet us at the station. She looked a little pale but every bit as handsome as I remembered her. With her on the platform was a young lady of quite extraordinary loveliness whom she introduced as Janos's cousin, Lucy Westenra. Mina told us that she was staying with Lucy while

Janos was away in Transylvania. I noticed that the very mention of his absence brought tears to her eyes but she rallied quickly and led the way to a waiting carriage. Holmes was taken with the vastness of the station, one of the largest in Europe and of great credit to the Empire.

We learned to our surprise that we too were to stay at the house of Lucy's father, Dr Josef Westenra. Holmes derived some amusement from the knowledge that Dr Westenra was the director of a lunatic asylum and that the house we were to stay in was just outside the grounds of the asylum.

The setting was quite remarkable, high on a hill overlooking Old Buda with a ruined abbey nearby, a most noble ruin with, of course, a legend attached.

It seemed that a white lady would appear at certain time at one of the windows.

An old graveyard full of tombstones lay below the house, giving splendid views of The Danube winding its way between the halves of the city, Buda and Pesht. The descent was quite steep in parts. Some of the lichen-covered gravestones had toppled over or collapsed into the graves.

Our host, Dr Westenra, had left that day to attend a conference in Vienna but he had given instructions that we were to be his guests and that he dearly hoped we would stay on until his return as he looked forward to making the acquaintance of Holmes and myself.

After a pleasant supper at which the serving girls bobbed prettily and endlessly as they went about their duties we settled by the fire and Mina began to tell us of her concern. Lucy sat quietly with her sewing but listened intently to Mina's story.

"Janos was so proud," Mina said. "It was his first personal transaction since he obtained his partnership with Herr Hofner. He had conducted the whole of the negotiations. Poor Herr Hofner, his death will be such a shock to Janos."

Holmes leaned forward attentively.

"Your husband's partner has passed away?"

Mina nodded sadly.

"Yes," she said in a hushed voice. "I decided to go to him when I became concerned about Janos. Imagine my horror. The cortege was just setting off from his house. The coffin was open. The street was lined with mourners.

I almost fainted. He was such a dear, dear man. To see him borne on the shoulders of those black-clad bearers, his white hair ruffled by the breeze, his face waxen pale ..."

"His death was unexpected?" Holmes asked solicitously.

Mina nodded agreement.

"His manservant heard a cry in the night. When he entered Herr Hofner's chamber he found his master dead, his face stricken, his arms above him as if fending off some terrible blow."

Mina turned away to stare into the fire. I was relieved when Holmes moved on to the matter of Janos's absence.

"Tell me about your husband's journey. What was it that first troubled you?"

Mina composed herself.

"He expected to be away for about a week. Ten days at the most, Mr Holmes. The area is apparently quite remote and transportation none too frequent. He was to be the Count's guest of course and expected to stay no more than a night or two. He was sure his paperwork was in order and it was really only a matter of signatures and perhaps minor amendments."

"Yes of course," murmured Holmes.

Mina's face brightened momentarily.

"He wrote to me from Klausenberg and again from Bistritz! Wonderful letters full of his thoughts and observations, amusing and ... and endearing. And then nothing until the end of the second week. Just when I felt sure he would walk through the door - another letter arrived. It was so strange ... so ... formal, simply saying he had been delayed. It was so cold, so remote ..."

She bit her lip to force back her tears.

"And that was the last time you heard from him?" inquired Holmes.

"No," she said, "there was another letter a week later ..."

"To the day?" asked Holmes.

"Yes," she replied, "to the day."

Holmes laid his pipe aside. "Do you think," he asked gently, "I might have sight of the correspondence?"

"Yes, of course," said Mina. She crossed to the door, where she hesitated.

"All of the letters, Mr Holmes?" she asked.

"I think it might be helpful," Holmes replied. "Your old uncle and I are men of the world and are not nearly so insensitive to the feelings of the young as you might suppose."

His smile obviously reassured her.

"They are in my room," she said, with a trace of a blush on her cheeks. She went out into the hall, closing the door quietly.

"Odd business," I murmured, "'expect there's some simple explanation ... snowed in or something of that sort."

Holmes ignored my remark.

"You are very intent upon your sewing, Miss Westenra," Holmes said pleasantly.

"Something quite intricate, it would seem."

Lucy appeared quite startled when she heard her name.

"I'm sorry," she said, "I was quite ... far away. This is ... for my trousseau ..."

"Splendid," Holmes declared. "A most worthy cause."

When my niece returned she and I talked of other things as Holmes set about his task, refilling and lighting his pipe as he did so. After a time he moved to a spot where the light was stronger. He took out his magnifying glass, peering closely at the correspondence. He interrupted our inconsequential chatter with an emphatic

"Harrumph!" and a shuffling of papers.

"There are one or two -" He broke off for a moment to glance at Mina's anxious face. "The later letters," he resumed in a somewhat softer voice, "have curious similarities. I have a fancy they were written on the same day."

"But why -" my niece began.

"The postmarks are certainly different but apart from the similarly formal tone, the penmanship is identical and yet not quite his normal hand. The flow is neither the same nor the angle. It is his hand and it is his signature, of that I have no doubt, but nevertheless the formality of the text is not the only troubling factor."

He folded the correspondence and returned it to Mina and said, "I think, young lady, it behoves your uncle and I to journey to Castle Dracula. Certainly, if anything is amiss, Count Dracula should be able to point us in the right direction."

Mina's gratitude and evident relief were infinitely touching but Holmes would have none of it.

"There is no urgent need for our return to London. I expect Scotland Yard feel somewhat at sea without me and it may well cause unhealthy excitement among the criminal classes but -"

He looked at me with a degree of eagerness and a suggestion of tension in his brightened eyes.

"- we can hardly continue upon our journey, don't you agree, my dear Watson, leaving your niece in such anxiety?"

I could hardly disagree since Mina had long held a special place in my affections.

Having consulted Baedeker and decided on a mid-morning departure we retired to our rooms.

I was awakened from a deep sleep in the early hours of the morning when Holmes, still in his smoking jacket, burst into my room, lamp in hand.

"Wake up, Watson," he declared, "there is something strange afoot." I struggled out of bed, still half asleep, groping for my robe and slippers as he went on.

"Our hostess, young Lucy, appears to be walking in her sleep. She is making for the graveyard."

"Good Lord," I said, getting my wits together, "she could fall to her death."

"Exactly," said Holmes. "Hurry, man, we must head her off!"

As we made for the stairs, Mina came hurrying onto the landing in her night attire.

"Is it Lucy?" she asked anxiously.

"Yes," declared Holmes, hurrying ahead, "she is walking in her sleep." Mina was close behind me as we ran out onto the lawn.

"This is the second time this week," Mina told me. "Poor dear, something is troubling her. She did this as a child. Her mother, too, was subject to it."

Holmes reached the lych-gate, which led to the graveyard. Mina and I were close on his heels. He indicated that we should spread out so as to encircle her. Lucy made her way slowly, arms outstretched, something ethereal about her movements almost as if she were floating among the gravestones. Holmes signalled that we should stop as Lucy paused and lay upon a stone bench overlooking the city below.

"Just as before!" Mina whispered to me. "It is our favourite spot. We sit there in the afternoons talking about the plans for her wedding next month. I think it is the excitement of it all that is disturbing her like this."

We approached her quietly, side-stepping the lichen-covered gravestones. Angels, arms outstretched, looked down upon us as we made our way toward her. There was a rapid fluttering of wings as a large bat-like creature appeared to hover above her before disappearing into a gathering mist.

"Shall I go to her?" Mina asked.

"Yes, yes," I said. "You will not alarm her."

I signalled our intention to Holmes who nodded agreement.

We remained in the shadows as Mina gently wakened Lucy and began to guide her back up to the house. The young woman looked pale but very beautiful in her long nightdress, her golden tresses tumbled about her shoulders. She seemed to be smiling but in a dreamy, trance-like state.

Holmes and I fell in together, giving Mina time to take Lucy into the house.

"Rum business," I said, stifling a yawn. "Seems it runs in the family."

"Hmm, decidedly rum," said Holmes, "and dangerous too."

"Indeed," I said as I took another look at the lights of the city below.

"Hear that?" asked Holmes.

It was only then that I became aware of the most awful howling and despairing cries coming from the neighbouring asylum.

"Poor, tormented souls," Holmes remarked.

"An asylum and a cemetery," I said with a chuckle, "hardly the most convivial spot in which to reside. Good thing you were awake by the way. What on earth kept you from your bed at such an hour?"

"I was reading up on our destination. Dr Westenra's library proved an excellent source."

"Your tirelessness is quite remarkable."

"One needs little sleep," he replied, "particularly when there is an interesting problem to be solved."

It was only then that I was reminded of the journey ahead. We reached the house and I was glad to shut out the mournful wailing of the lunatics.

In the morning my niece prevailed upon the cook to produce a good English breakfast. Lucy, the dutiful hostess, came down to join us but I thought that despite her ethereal charm she looked a little pale. I noticed that Mina kept her eyes on the window overlooking the drive and she hastily excused herself when she sighted the approach of the local postman. She was quite cast down when she returned to the breakfast room but put on a brave face and stoutly protested when we insisted that it was not necessary for the young ladies to accompany us to the station.

A coach was summoned. Both Holmes and I gave assurances that we looked forward to a longer stay on our return.

"If Janos returns before us, and he may well," said Holmes, "we will have had the opportunity to see something of this beautiful country and then can explore the city itself."

Mina seemed cheered by the thought as she and Lucy waved us goodbye.

"Do you think it is likely that the young man may return before us?" I asked as the coach and pair trundled down the drive.

"I fear not," he replied nestling in silence into his heavy coat.

CHAPTER TWO

Our journey to Klausenberg passed pleasantly enough though the train lacked the sophistication of the Transcontinental Express.

We stayed the night at The Hotel Royal, a comfortable hostelry not quite as resplendent as its name implied. We dined on chicken heavily spiced with red pepper, inducing a thirst for some excellent Tokay. It is, apparently, a national dish called 'Paprika Hendl'.

Holmes had acquired maps of the country, locating the district we were bound for in the extreme east, on the borders of three states; Transylvania, Moldavia and Bukovina in the midst of the Carpathian mountains, evidently one of the wildest and least known portions of Europe. We could find no trace of an exact location for Castle Dracula, as there were no maps as yet to compare with our own Ordnance Surveys, but we found that Bistritz, the post town named in Janos's letters, was quite a well-known place.

As usual Holmes had done a considerable amount of research and it was that which had kept him reading far into the previous night.

Over our meal he gave me a lengthy discourse on Transylvania. It seems that in the population there are four different nationalities:

Saxons in the south, and mixed with them the Wallachs, who are descendants of the Daciens, Magyars in the west and Szekelys in the east and north. We were going to the latter, who claim to be descended from Attila and the Huns. When the Magyars conquered the country in the eleventh century they found The Huns settled in it.

I did not sleep well, though my bed was comfortable enough, for I had all sorts of odd dreams. There was a dog howling all night under my window, which may have had something to do with my unease; or it may have been the paprika.

Needless to say, Holmes reported in the morning that he had slept soundly and was already breakfasting when I entered our sitting room. The meal contained more paprika, a sort of porridge of maize flour, which the waiter said was 'mamaliga', and eggplant stuffed with forcemeat, a tasty dish that he called 'implatata'.

I had to hurry, as our train was due to leave at eight o'clock. In fact it was more than an hour after we boarded before the train began to move. It seems that the further east one travels the more unpunctual are the trains.

All day long we seemed to dawdle through countryside full of beauty of every kind. Sometimes we saw little towns or castles on the top of steep hills such as one sees illustrated in old missals; sometimes we ran by rivers and streams which seemed from the wide stony margin on each side of them to be subject to great floods. It takes a lot of water, and running strong, to sweep the outside edge of a river clear.

At every station there were groups of people in all sorts of attire. Some of them were just like country folk at home, or those we saw travelling through France and Germany, with short jackets and round hats and homemade trousers; but others were very picturesque. The women looked pretty, except when you got near them, but they were very clumsy about the waist. They had all full white sleeves of some kind or another, and most of them had big belts with a lot of strips of something fluttering from them like the dresses in a ballet, but of course with petticoats under them.

The strangest figures were the Slovaks, who looked more barbarian than the rest, with their big cowboy hats, great baggy dirty-white trousers, white linen shirts and enormous heavy belts, nearly a foot wide, all studded over with brass nails. They wore high boots with their trousers tucked into them and had long black hair and heavy black moustaches. Holmes remarked that on stage they would be set down at once as some wandering band of brigands and his imagery put me in mind of pleasant evenings at Drury Lane. He brought me abruptly back to the present with a curious observation on our brief sojourn in Budapest.

"Somnambulism is a strange phenomena," he mused, gazing out at the wild and desolate countryside. "Luther held that dreams, visions and somnambulism are frequently caused by Satan, plaguing and tormenting people in all manner of ways. Some he affrights in their sleep, with heavy dreams and visions, so that the whole body sweats in anguish of heart. Some he leads, sleeping, out of their beds and chambers up into high, dangerous places, so that if, by the loving angels about them, they were not preserved, he would throw them down and cause their death."

"Whatever put you in mind of that?" I asked.

"On the other hand," he continued, ignoring my interruption, "the papists say that sleep-walkers are persons who have not been baptised; or, if they have been, that the priest was drunk when he administered the Sacrament!"

This last produced the ghost of a smile on his pale countenance.

"It is strange is it not that this vast expanse," he resumed, waving a hand at the passing scene, "evokes in you a picture of fairy-tale castles and tranquil lives of simple peasant folk, while in me it creates a feeling of isolation and of the impunity with which crime may be committed there."

"Good Heavens!" I declared. "Who would associate crime with such a glorious setting?"

"Such scenes often fill me with horror," he said. "It is one of the curses of a mind with a turn like mine that I must look at everything with reference to my own special subject. It is my belief, Watson, founded upon experience, that the lowest and vilest alleys of the city do not present a more dreadful record of sin than does the smiling and beautiful countryside."

"You horrify me!" I said.

"But the reason is very obvious. The pressure of public opinion can do in the town what the law cannot accomplish. There is no lane so vile that the scream of a tortured child, or the thud of a drunkard's blow, does not beget sympathy and indignation among the neighbours, and then the whole machinery of justice is ever so close that a word of complaint can set it going, and there is but a step between the crime and the dock. But look at those lonely hovels, each in its own fields, filled for the most part with poor ignorant folk who know little of the law.

Think of the deeds of hellish cruelty, the hidden wickednesses which may go on, year in, year out, in such places, and none the wiser."

I looked out into the gathering gloom where a few peasants were making their way home after a long day in the fields. One prayed that they were too weary to think of deeds of hellish cruelty or of hidden wickednesses.

It was on the dark side of twilight when we got to Bistritz, which is a very interesting old place. Being practically on the border - for the Borgo Pass leads from it into Bukovina - it has had a very stormy existence, and it certainly shows marks of it. Fifty years ago a series of great fires caused havoc on five separate occasions. At the beginning of the seventeenth century it underwent a siege and lost thirteen thousand people, the casualties of war proper being assisted by famine and disease.

We had wired ahead for rooms at The Golden Krone Hotel, which we found to be delightfully old-fashioned and very typical of the area.

HoImes and I were taken by surprise when the Landlord produced a letter addressed to "The English Herren", which, upon opening, we found to be from Count Dracula!

"How the devil did he know of our arrival?" I asked. HoImes sat calmly in a huge old leather chair and read the letter to me:

"Gentlemen: Welcome to The Carpathians. I am anxiously expecting you and know of your concerns. Sleep well tonight. At three tomorrow the diligence will start for Bukovina; places will be kept for you. At The Borgo Pass my carriage will await you and bring you to me. Your friend, Dracula."

"The bush telegraph seems to be in good order," Holmes remarked dryly, throwing a glance at the Landlord who was busy with preparations for the evening meal.

We dined on what they call "Robber Steak" - bits of bacon, onion and beef, seasoned with red pepper, strung on sticks and roasted over the fire, in the simple style of the London cat's meat! The wine was Golden Mediasch, which produces a queer sting to the tongue, but otherwise quite agreeable.

I noticed one or two of our fellow diners giving us curious glances. The Landlady, who served us, seemed to look upon my friend and I with a degree of pity.

We overheard one or two remarks that seemed to refer to us. Holmes, using his polyglot dictionary; interpreted with some amusement. He informed me that the word "Ordog" meant Satan, "Pokol" hell; "stregoica" witch; and that the words "vrolok" and "vlkoslak" had the same meaning in both Slovak and Serbian for something that is either werewolf or vampire. I felt a distinct unease but Holmes set his little book aside and gave his attention to a substantial strudel.

When I was dressing next morning The Landlady came to my room. She was a buxom woman with a kindly, careworn face. She seemed agitated and whispered urgently as if anxious not to be overheard. She crossed herself several times and pleaded with me in broken English. "No go, Englishmen. No, to-day bad, very bad ..."

I tried to reason with her, explaining that my friend and I were on urgent business.

"Tonight is St George's Eve!" she declared, crossing herself again. "Tonight when midnight ... all evil things abroad. You go to Castle Dracula! Bad! Very bad ..."

More signs of the cross and a muttered prayer. Then she kissed the crucifix about her neck, removed it and offered it to me. Despite my protests she placed it over my head, tucked it under my shirt and closed the buttons over it.

She begged me not to remove it, to wear it at all times. I did not know what to do, for, as an English churchman, I had been taught to regard such things as in some measure idolatrous, and yet it seemed so ungracious to refuse her when she meant well and was in such a state of mind.

I thanked her profusely, she curtsied and backed away, still distressed but able to muster a slight, sad smile.

At that moment Holmes was about to enter. She crossed herself once more and hurried away. Holmes closed the door after her with a chuckle. "I suppose she has been bothering you with all that nonsense about what will happen on the stroke of midnight. I gave her short shrift I can tell you!"

I fingered the crucifix under my shirt and decided not to admit my foolishness.

When we were preparing to board the coach I noted that The Landlord was in earnest conversation with the driver. It was evident that they were discussing Holmes and I because there were frequent looks in our direction. Some of the local people were sitting on a bench by the entrance to the inn. They, too, were intent upon observing us and I heard again some of those curious words used in the dining room.

As the coach moved off the locals, who by now had swelled to a crowd of two dozen or more, all made the sign of the cross and pointed menacingly. With some difficulty I got a fellow-passenger to tell me what was going on. At first he would not answer me, seeming as discomfited by our presence as the other passengers, but grudgingly muttered something about "the evil eye." Holmes smiled, evidently finding a certain charm in such quaint beliefs. Our departure was certainly picturesque. The cobbled yard of the inn was lined with the rich foliage of oleander with orange trees in green tubs clustered in the centre.

Our driver, whose wide linen drawers covered the whole front of the box seat, cracked his whip over his four small horses, which ran abreast, and I soon lost any recollection of ghostly fears in the beauty of the scene as we drove along. Holmes, however, understood some of the language, or rather languages, of our fellow-passengers and intimated that there was more folklore about the eve of St George's Day in their somewhat furtive discussions.

Before us lay a green sloping land full of forests and woods with here and there farmhouses on hillsides, their blank gable ends to the road. There was everywhere a bewildering mass of fruit blossom - apple, plum, pear, cherry; and as we drove by I could see the green grass under the trees spangled with the fallen petals. In and out amongst the green hills of the "Mittel Land" ran the road, losing itself as it swept round the grassy curve, or shut out by the straggling ends of pine woods, running down the hillsides like tongues of flame.

The road was rugged but we seemed to fly over it with a feverish haste. Puzzling and somewhat uncomfortable until Holmes informed me that the driver was bent on losing no time in reaching Borgo Prund.

"Apparently this road in summer-time is excellent," he told me," but it has not yet been put in order after the winter snows."

"I see," I said, easing my stiffening buttocks.

"In this respect it is different from the general run of the roads in The Carpathians," he went on, enjoying the opportunity to air his gathering knowledge of the country, "for it was an old tradition that they were not to be kept in too good order, lest The Turks should think The Hospadars were preparing for war!"

Beyond the green swelling hills of the Mittel Land rose mighty slopes of forests up to the lofty steeps of The Carpathians themselves. Right and left of us they towered, with the afternoon sun full upon them, bringing out all the glorious colours of this beautiful range, deep blue and purple in the shadows of the peaks, green and brown where grass and rock mingled, and an endless perspective of jagged rocks and pointed crags, till these were themselves lost in the distance where the snowy peaks rose grandly. Here and there seemed mighty rifts in the mountains, through which, as the sun began to sink, we saw now and again the white gleam of falling water.

One of the passengers touched my arm as the road swept around the base of a hill revealing the lofty snowy peak of a mountain.

"Look!" he said. "Isten szek! God's seat!" Then he crossed himself reverently.

As we wound our endless way and the sun sank lower and lower behind us, the shadows of evening began to creep around us. Here and there we passed Cszeks and Slovaks, all in colourful attire but I noticed the goitre was painfully prevalent. By the roadsides were many small shrines and as we swept by, our companions crossed themselves. Peasant men and women knelt before the shrines; they did not turn around as we passed, as if in the self-surrender of devotion, having neither eyes nor ears for the outer world.

There were many things new to me; hayricks in trees, beautiful masses of weeping birch, their white stems shining like silver through the delicate green of the leaves. Now and again we passed a leiter-wagon drawn by a shaggy horse, the cart's long, snake-like vertebra calculated to suit the inequalities of the road.

On this were sure to be seated a group of home-going peasants, the men carrying their long staves topped with axe-heads.

As evening fell it began to get very cold. The growing twilight merged into one dark mistiness, the trees, oak, beech and pine, in deepening gloom, though in the valleys which ran deep between the spurs of the hills, as we ascended through the Pass, the dark firs stood out against the background of late-lying snow.

Sometimes, as the road cut through the pine woods that seemed in the darkness to be closing down upon us, great masses of greyness produced a weird and solemn effect, begetting grim fancies.

In places the hills were so steep that, despite our driver's haste, the horses could only go up slowly. Holmes shouted to the driver that we should walk up them as we would at home but the man would have none of it.

"No, no, you must not walk here, the dogs are too fierce," he cried and then added with what was meant for grim pleasantry - for he looked round to catch the approving smiles of the rest - "and you may have enough of such matters before you go to sleep."

The only stop he would make was a short pause to light his lamps.

As time passed there seemed to be some excitement amongst our fellow-passengers. They kept calling to the driver, one after the other, as though urging him to further speed. He lashed the horses unmercifully with his long whip and with wild cries of encouragement urged them on to further exertions.

Then through the darkness I could see a patch of grey light ahead of us, as though there was a great cleft in the hills. The excitement of the passengers grew greater; the coach rocked crazily on its great leather springs, swaying like a boat tossed on a stormy sea. We had to hold on. The road grew more level and we appeared to fly along. The mountains seemed to come nearer to us on each side as if frowning upon us. We were entering The Borgo Pass.

On each side the passengers peered eagerly into the darkness. It was evident something very exciting was expected. This state of excitement kept up for some little time but Holmes made nothing of it, evidently lost in some meditation of his own.

At last we saw the pass opening up on the eastern side. There were dark, rolling clouds overhead, and in the air the heavy, oppressive sense of thunder as if the mountain range had separated two atmospheres and now we were in the thunderous one.

I was looking out for the conveyance that would take us to the Count. Any moment I expected to see the glare of lamps through the blackness but all was darkness, the only light coming from the flickering rays of our own lamps, in which the steam of our hard-driven horses rose in a white cloud.

The passengers drew back with a sigh of gladness when the driver, looking at his timepiece, said something to the others.

"An hour less than time," Holmes reported to me, adding dryly "Hardly surprising."

The driver turned to Holmes and said, "The herren are not expected after all. You will come on to Bukovina and return tomorrow or the next day; better the next day."

Whilst he was speaking and before Holmes or I could protest, the horses began to neigh and snort and plunge wildly, so that the driver had to hold them up.

Then, amongst a chorus of screams and much crossing of themselves, a caleche drawn by a pair of fine horses, raced up behind us, overtaking and hauling alongside. I could see from the flash of our lamps that the horses were coal-black, splendid beasts. They were driven by a man in a great black coat and hat, which mostly hid his face from us. I could see only the gleam of a pair of very bright eyes, reddened in the lamplight, as he turned to our driver.

"You are early tonight, my friend."

"The Herr Englishmen were in a hurry," the driver stammered in reply.

"That is why, I suppose," the man said icily, "you wished them to go on to Bukovina? You cannot deceive me. I know too much and my horses are swift."

As he spoke he smiled, the lamplight fell on a hard-looking mouth with very red lips and sharp teeth as white as ivory. One of the passengers whispered to another "Denn die Todten reiten schnell."

Holmes, preparing to alight, translated for me: "'For the Dead travel fast'. A line from Burger's 'Lenore'."

The strange driver evidently heard the words for he looked up, his smile frozen in a rictus grin. The passenger who had spoken turned his face away, at the same time putting two fingers together and crossing himself.

As we boarded our new transport the driver called to us: "There is a flask of slivovitz underneath the seat should you require it. The night is chill and my Master, the Count, bade me take all care of you."

He shook his reins, the horses turned, and we swept into the darkness of The Pass. As I looked back I saw the steam from the horses of the coach by the light of the lamps, and projected against it the figures of our late companions. Then their driver cracked his whip and called to his horses and off they went on their way to Bukovina.

We drew great rugs about ourselves and Holmes retrieved the flask and offered it to me. I accepted willingly enough since the chill struck an odd sense of loneliness into my very vitals. Holmes declined and replaced the flask.

"Slivovitz is a little too fiery for my taste," he said.

"True enough," I thought. It was as though I had lit a fire in my stomach. The carriage went at a hard pace. We seemed to have travelled for quite some time when Holmes leaned forward to me and said quietly:

"Have you noticed that we are travelling in circles?"

Now that he had said it, I did recall that one or two landmarks had begun to look somewhat familiar.

"Do you know," I said, "I believe you are right."

"I am," Holmes replied dryly.

I struck a match and by its flame looked at my watch. It was close to midnight.

"It is almost twelve," I said.

"Quite so," said Holmes, "quite so."

I suppose the general superstition about midnight had been increased by these recent experiences. I have to admit that I waited with a queasy feeling of suspense.

A dog began to howl somewhere - in a farmhouse perhaps - a long, agonised wailing as if from fear. It was taken up by another dog, then another and another, till, borne upon the wind, a wild howling seemed to come from all over the countryside as far as the imagination could grasp it through the gloom of the night. At the first howl the horses began to strain and rear, but the driver spoke to them soothingly and they quieted down.

Then far off in the distance, from the mountains on each side of us, there came a louder and sharper howling.

"Wolves!" said Holmes, his ears attuned to the change.

"Heavens, man," I said, "it reminds me of Grimpen Moor."

"This is a far cry from the hound of the Baskervilles," he replied evenly, peering out into the darkness.

Now the horses reared and plunged madly and the driver had to use all his strength to keep them from bolting. But, as our ears became accustomed to the sound, the horses so far became quiet that the driver was able to descend and stand before them. He stroked and soothed them, whispering in their ears as I have heard of horse-tamers doing, and with extraordinary effect, for under his caresses they became quite manageable again, though they still trembled. The driver again took his seat and shook his reins, starting off at a great pace.

This time, after going down the far side of The Pass, he suddenly turned down a narrow roadway, which ran sharply to the right.

Soon we were hemmed in with trees, which in places arched right over the roadway till we passed as through a tunnel; and again great frowning rocks guarded us boldly on either side. Though we were in shelter, we could hear the rising wind, for it moaned and whistled through the rocks, and the branches of trees crashed together as we swept along. It grew colder and colder still. Fine, powdery snow began to fall, laying a soft blanket all around us. The keen wind still carried the howling of the dogs though this grew fainter. The baying of the wolves sounded nearer and nearer as though they were closing on us from every side.

I have to admit I was afraid. Holmes was as inscrutable as ever. Certainly the horses shared my fear but the driver was not in the least disturbed. Suddenly Holmes pointed to something away on our left and I looked in that direction. There was a faint flickering blue flame.

The driver must have seen it at the same moment for he checked the horses, jumped to the ground and disappeared into the darkness.

"What on earth is going on?" I asked my friend.

"Whatever it is," Holmes replied, "I think it would be unwise to tempt the wolves by following him."

"Humph," I said, thinking it over. Then the driver reappeared and without a word took his seat and we resumed our journey.

This happened several times. On one occasion the flame appeared so near the road that even in the darkness we could watch the driver's movements. He went rapidly to where the blue flame arose - it must have been very faint for it did not seem to illumine the area around it - and gathering a few stones formed them into some device.

Once when he stood between us and the flame, it appeared that he did not obstruct it, for we could see the ghostly flicker all the same.

"Odd, Holmes," I murmured, "do you see that?"

"A strange trick of the light," he observed, "a most unusual optical effect."

I took it that our eyes were deceiving us, straining to see through the darkness.

For a time there were no blue flames and we sped on through the gloom with the howling of the wolves accompanying us. When the next one appeared somewhat further afield the driver leapt from his seat and hurried away. During his absence the horses began to snort and scream with fright. At first I could not see any cause for it as the wolves had ceased their howling. But the moon, sailing through black clouds, appeared behind the jagged crest of a beetling, pine-clad rock and by its light we saw around us a ring of wolves with white teeth and lolling red tongues, long sinewy limbs and shaggy hair. They were a hundred times more terrifying in the grim silence. For myself, I felt a paralysis of fear. It is only when a man finds himself face-to-face with such horrors that he can understand their true import.

"Don't move," said Holmes quietly. "Be still, absolutely still."

All at once the wolves began to howl again as though the moonlight had some peculiar effect upon them. We held on as the horses jumped about and reared, their eyes rolling in a way painful to see. The living ring of terror encompassed them on all sides and they had, perforce, to remain within it.

Suddenly the coachman reappeared. We heard his voice raised in a hissing command. He swept his long arms as though brushing aside some impalpable obstacle and the wolves fell back and back. A heavy cloud passed over the face of the moon and we were again in darkness as he took his seat, shook the reins, and we set off once more.

The time seemed interminable as we travelled on in complete darkness for the rolling clouds completely obscured the moon. We climbed higher and higher along a narrow winding road until I realised that we were arriving in the courtyard of a vast, half-ruined castle, from whose tall black windows came no ray of light. "It seems," murmured Holmes, "that we have arrived ..."

CHAPTER THREE

When the caleche stopped the driver jumped down and held out a hand to assist us. Again I could not but notice his prodigious strength. His hand actually seemed like a steel vice that could have crushed mine if he had chosen. Then he took out our traps and placed them beside us as we stood by a great door, old and studded with iron nails, and set in a projecting doorway of massive stone. I could see in the dim light that the door was ornately carved but that the carving had been much worn by time and weather.

The driver jumped up again into his seat and shook the reins; the horses started forward, and the carriage disappeared down one of several openings under great round arches. In the gloom the courtyard looked of considerable size.

I struck a match and held it up.

"Do you see a bell-pull or a knocker?" I asked.

Holmes shook his head. I raised my cane and gave the door a couple of sharp raps.

There was silence except for the sighing of the wind and a faint fluttering sound somewhere above.

I rapped on the door again but there was no response. Holmes stepped back into the courtyard and looked up at the frowning walls and dark window openings.

"They are abed, servants and all," he said before calling out "Hulloa!" a couple of times, his voice echoing around the courtyard.

Then we waited and I flexed my arms to ward off the damp and eerie chill of the place.

From within we heard the sound of a slow, heavy step approaching behind the great door and saw through the chinks the gleam of an approaching light. Then there was a sound of rattling chains and clanking of massive bolts drawn back. A key was turned with the loud grating noise of long disuse, and the door swung back on creaking hinges. Within, stood a tall old man, clad in black from head to foot, without a single speck of colour about him anywhere.

He motioned us in with a courtly gesture, saying in excellent English, but with a strange intonation:

"Welcome to my house. Come freely. Go safely. And leave something of the happiness you bring!"

Holmes glanced at me and stepped over the threshold. The instant he moved, the old man grasped his hand and mine, too, as I followed.

"Welcome! Welcome!" he said, his face solemn and unsmiling. His grip had a strength that made me wince, not lessened by the fact that it seemed as cold as ice – more like the hand of a dead rather than a living man.

The strength of the handshake was so akin to that which I had noticed in the driver, whose face I had only seen dimly, that for a moment I doubted if it were not the same person.

"Count Dracula?" I asked.

"I am Dracula," he replied.

I introduced my friend and myself. The Count made no sign that he recognised either of our names but busied himself, despite our protests, in taking in our luggage.

"The night air is chill," he said, "you need food and rest. It is late and my people are not available. Let me see to your comfort myself."

He led the way up a great winding stair, and along a passage, on whose stone floor our steps rang heavily. At the end of this he threw open a heavy door which was the entrance to a large candle-lit room in which a table was spread for supper and on whose mighty hearth a fire of logs flamed and flared.

We passed through this room into another stone passage leading to our rooms.

"You will need to refresh yourselves," he said solemnly. "When you are ready you will find your supper prepared."

He shuffled away down the passage. The rooms were large and well-lighted and both had log fires which crackled and spat in their hearths.

Holmes moved around the rooms with evident purpose, looking out of the windows at the darkness below.

"We are in the east wing," he said thoughtfully, "I fancy it is a sheer drop below. The castle is, I think, built on the edge of a cliff."

"Really?" I said for I could see little myself.

I busied myself with my toilet as I realised I was half-famished with hunger.

"Our driver moved swiftly to change his garb and greet us so speedily," he remarked as he returned to his own room.

"You think so, too –" I began but my friend had closed his door.

Supper was already laid out when we returned to the dining hall. Our host stood on one side of the great fireplace. Leaning against the stone-work, he made a graceful wave of his hand to the table and said:

"I pray you be seated and sup how you please. You will, I trust, excuse me that I do not join you; but I have dined already, and I do not sup."

We settled ourselves in the great oaken chairs and the Count himself came forward and took off the cover of a dish containing an excellent roast chicken. We dined off that and cheese and salad and drank a bottle of old Tokay.

As we supped the Count asked us about Budapest, a city of which he was not acquainted but which greatly interested him. Holmes explained that we could tell him little since we had only spent a few hours there. He was about to broach the subject of our visit when the Count asked him about our journey to the castle.

"Greatly facilitated by your kind intervention," Holmes replied. "We were not aware that you had been informed of our intention to visit you."

"But you come about the young man, do you not?" the Count asked, looking from one of us to the other. "His employers commissioned you? They wrote of their concern?"

"No, sir," I said. "We are here on behalf of my niece, the wife of the young gentleman."

His eyes flickered for a moment.

"A strange business," he said. "He left here some time ago, our transactions completed."

"Did he board the diligence to Bistritz?" Holmes enquired.

"That I cannot tell you," the Count answered. "I was absent at the time. He left abruptly and I was somewhat surprised."

"But how would he get back –" I began.

"Perhaps he obtained passage from the local peasants," he said. He changed the subject and engaged my friend in more questions about Budapest. While they talked I had the opportunity to observe him more closely. His face was a strong – a very strong – aquiline, with high bridge of the thin nose and peculiarly arched nostrils; with lofty domed forehead, and hair growing scantily round the temples but profusely elsewhere. His eyebrows were massive, almost meeting over the nose, and with bushy hair that seemed to curl in its own profusion. The mouth was fixed and rather cruel-looking, with peculiarly sharp white teeth; these protruded over the lips, whose remarkable ruddiness showed astonishing vitality in a man of his years. For the rest, his ears were pale and at the tops extremely pointed; the chin was broad and strong, and the cheeks firm though thin. The general effect was one of extraordinary pallor.

Hitherto I had noticed the backs of his hands had seemed rather white and fine but as he gestured during his conversation with Holmes I noticed that they were rather coarse – broad, with squat fingers. Strange to say, there were hairs in the centre of the palm. The nails were long and fine, and cut to a sharp point. When he rose to lean over me to replenish my glass, I could not repress a shudder. It may have been that his breath was rank, but a horrible feelings of nausea came over me, which, do what I would, I could not conceal. The Count, evidently noticing it, drew back with a grim sort of smile, which showed more than he had yet done of his protuberant teeth.

As he settled himself after serving us both there came the sound of wolves howling in the valley. The Count's eyes gleamed, and he said:

"Listen to them – the children of the night. What music they make!"

"We encountered them on our journey," Holmes remarked. "Indeed," he went on, "your coachman seemed to have remarkable power over them."

The Count, ignoring this, replied: "You chose a strange night for your journey. It is believed hereabouts that on St George's Eve all evil spirits have unchecked sway. Did you not see the little blue flames?"

"Yes!" I said. "Your driver was greatly taken with them."

"They are said to signal the places where treasure has been concealed," he said. "That treasure has been hidden in the region there can be but little doubt; for it was the ground fought over for centuries by the Wallachian, the Saxon and the Turk. There is hardly a foot of soil in all this region that has not been enriched by the blood of men, patriots or invaders. In old days there were stirring times, when the Austrian and the Hungarian came up in hordes, and the patriots went out to meet them – men and women, the aged and the children too – and waited their coming on the rocks above the passes, that they might sweep destruction on them with their artificial avalanches. When the invader was triumphant he found but little, for whatever there was had been sheltered in the friendly soil."

"But how," asked Holmes, evidently humouring the man, "can it have remained so long undiscovered when there is a sure index to it if men will but take the trouble to look?"

"Because," replied the Count, "your peasant is at heart a coward and a fool! Those flames only appear on one night. And on that night no man of this land will, if he can help it, stir without his doors. And, dear sir, even if he did he would not know what to do."

Turning to me, he went on:

"Why, the peasant that you tell me of, my servant, would not know where to look in daylight even if he marked the place."

"That he did, sir, with some care," I said.

Holmes was lighting his pipe, far more relaxed than I in this strange place and in the menacing presence of our host.

"I am sure your family were in the vanguard of the patriots in those fearsome times," said Holmes.

This evidently pleased the Count for he warmed to the subject wonderfully. In his speaking of things and people, and especially of battles, he spoke as if he had been present at them all, explaining that to a boyar the pride of his house and name is his own pride, that their glory is his glory, that their fate is his fate. Whenever he spoke of his house he always said "we", in the plural, like a king.

Holmes seemed to have set aside the matter of the missing Janos for he seemed intent on hearing more of the history of the Draculas and the old man's reddened eyes glowed as he recalled episodes from the past.

"We Szekeleys have a right to be proud," he said, "for in our veins flows the blood of many brave races who fought as the lion fights, for lordship. Here, in the whirlpool of European races, the Ugric tribe bore down from Iceland the fighting spirit which Thor and Wodin gave them, which their Berserkers displayed to such fell intent on the seaboards of Europe, aye, and of Asia and Africa, too, till the peoples thought that the werewolves themselves had come."

Holmes eyes seemed to narrow to mere slits as he nodded agreeably.

The Count went on:

"Here, too, when they came, they found the Huns, whose warlike fury had swept the earth like a living flame, till the dying peoples held that in their veins ran the blood of those old witches, who, expelled from Scythia, had mated with the devils in the desert. Fools, fools! What devil or what witch was ever so great as Attila, whose blood is in these veins?"

He held up his arms in an attitude of triumph. I stared at Holmes who appeared to look right through me as the old man resumed his arrogant tirade:

"Is it a wonder that we were a conquering race; that we were proud; that when the Magyar, the Lombard, the Avar, the Bulgar or the Turk poured his thousands on our frontiers, we drove them back? Is it strange that when Arpad and his legions swept through the Hungarian fatherland he found us here when he reached the frontier; that the Honfoglasas was completed there? And when the Hungarian flood swept eastward, the Szekeleys were claimed as kindred by the victorious Magyars, and to us for centuries was trusted the guarding of the frontier of Turkeyland; aye, and more than that, endless duty of the frontier guard, for, as the Turks say, 'water sleeps, and enemy is sleepless.' Who more gladly than we throughout the Four Nations received the 'blood sword' or at its warlike call flocked quicker to the standard of The King? When was redeemed that great shame of my nation, the shame of Cassova, when the flags of the Wallach and the Magyar went down beneath the Crescent; who was it but one of my own race who as Voivode crossed the Danube and beat the Turk on his own ground!"

His eyes bore down on us as he went on:

"This was a Dracula! Was it not a Dracula who in a later age again and again brought his forces into Turkey-land? Who, when he was beaten back, came again and again, though he had come alone from the bloody field where his troops were being slaughtered, since he knew that he alone could ultimately triumph?"

The Count shook his head. "They said," he went on quietly, "that he thought only of himself. Bah! What good are peasants without a leader? Where ends the war without a brain and heart to conduct it? Again when, after the battle of the Mohacs, we threw off the Hungarian yoke, we of the Dracula blood were amongst their leaders, for our spirit would not brook that we were not free. The Szekeleys – and the Draculas as their heart's blood, their brains and their swords – can boast a record that mushroom growths like the Hapsburgs and the Romanoffs can never reach. The warlike days are over. Blood is too precious a thing in these days of dishonourable peace; and the glories of the great races are as a tale that is told."

He turned away and with his boot prodded at the dying embers of the fire.

"I suggest you sleep now, gentlemen," he said quietly with his back to us, "and tomorrow I will send my servants to enquire in the district of your missing friend."

With this he left us. Holmes gathered up his pipe and his pouch and took a candelabra from the table and waited for me to do the same. "Extraordinary fellow," I murmured.

"Extraordinary and mad, quite, quite evilly mad," said my friend, leading the way back to our rooms.

CHAPTER FOUR

Whatever unease I felt was lessened by sheer fatigue. I was about to climb into bed when Holmes entered my room still fully clothed and carrying a small torch.

"I think it might be well to get the lie of the land before we retire," he said. With some reluctance I dragged on my robe and proceeded to follow him.

We moved quietly along the stone passage, listening carefully for any sounds of movement but apart from the soft moaning of the wind outside there was silence. Holmes tried several doors but found them firmly locked. We passed through the dining hall to the winding stone steps and ascended to the battlements. Here again our way was barred but we were able to enter one of the look-out towers.

The thunderous clouds had cleared and the moon shone with a cold brightness. From the narrow apertures we could see far below. Holmes was about to move when something caught his eye.

"Look, Watson!" he declared, "there is something moving there!"

I followed the direction of his pointing and could dimly discern someone or something emerging from a mullioned window below and beginning to crawl, face down, with something like a cloak spread out like wings. The figure moved in lizard fashion sideways and downwards using handholds and footholds in every projection and inequality to move swiftly until it reached a hole or window far below, disappearing within.

"Good heavens!" I said, "what manner of creature is that?"

"I fancy it is our host," replied Holmes.

"But to scale a wall face down – "

"We need to see it in daylight," said Holmes, "but, meanwhile, since I believe he has left the castle and, I am sure, his talk of servants is nonsense, we can continue our search without fear of discovery."

We found our way back to the great door to the courtyard. With some difficulty we pulled back the bolts rusted and stiff with age and disuse and unhooked the chains but the door was locked and there was no sign of a key.

Continuing our search through passages and backstairs we tried door after door but all were firmly secured until at the top of a narrow stairway we came upon a door which, though it seemed to be locked, gave a little under pressure. Trying harder, we found it was not really locked but that the resistance came from the fact that the hinges had fallen somewhat and the heavy door rested on the floor.

We entered to find that we were now in a wing of the castle further to the right than our own accommodations. We were in a suite of rooms in the south wing of the castle, the windows of the end room looking out both west and south. On the latter side, as well as to the former, there was a precipice. The castle was built on the corner of a great rock so that on three sides it was quite impregnable, and large windows were placed here where sling and bow and culverin could not reach, and consequently light and comfort, impossible to a position which had to be guarded, were secured. In the moonlight we could discern that there was a great valley and, rising far away, the dim outlines of jagged mountain fastnesses.

Holmes searched the rooms as best he could with the aid of his slim torch and the yellow moonlight, flooding in through the diamond panes, but a wealth of dust lay over all and disguised in some measure the ravages of time and the moth. As with other parts of the castle there was a dread loneliness about the place which chilled the heart.

After a time Holmes gave up, deciding that it was better to continue our searches in daylight.

Finally, I lay on my bed, recalling with disbelief the events of the past few hours until I fell asleep. I woke with a start once or twice, but sleep overcame me until I seemed to be in a strange dream, half-waking, half-sleeping.

In the moonlight filtering through the window panes were three young women, ladies by their dress and manner. Two were dark, and had high aquiline noses, like the Count's, and great dark, piercing eyes, that seemed to be almost red when contrasted with the pale yellow moon. The other was fair, as fair as can be, with great wavy masses of golden hair and eyes like pale sapphires.

I seemed somehow to know her face, and to know it in connection with some weird prescience, but I could not recollect how or where.

All three had brilliant white teeth that shone like pearls against the ruby of their voluptuous lips. There was something about them that instilled in me a longing and at the same time a deadly fear. They whispered together, and they all three laughed, a silvery, musical laugh, yet so hard that the sound could not come through the softness of human lips. It was like the intolerable, tingling sweetness of water glasses when played on by a cunning hand.

The fair girl shook her head coquettishly and the other two urged her on.

"You are first," said one, "and we shall follow; yours is the right to begin."

"He is strong," said the other, "there are kisses for us all."

The fair girl advanced and bent over me till I could feel the movement of her breath upon me. Sweet it seemed in one sense, honey-sweet, but with a bitter underlying the sweet, a bitter offensiveness, as one smells in blood. I seemed unable to raise my eyelids, but looked out and saw perfectly under the lashes. The fair girl bent over me, fairly gloating. There was a deliberate voluptuousness which was both thrilling and repulsive and, as she arched her neck, she licked her lips like an animal. I could see the moisture shining on the scarlet lips and on the red tongue as it lapped the sharp white teeth. Lower and lower went her head as the lips went below the range of my mouth and chin and seemed about to fasten on my throat. Then she paused and I could hear the churning sound of her tongue as it licked her teeth and lips, and could feel the hot breath on my neck. Then the skin on my throat began to tingle. I could feel the soft, shivering touch of the lips on my throat and the hard dents of two sharp teeth, just touching and pausing there.

But at that instant, another sensation seemed to sweep through me. I felt the presence of the Count, and of his being as if lapped in a storm of fury. His strong hand grasped the slender neck of the fair woman and with giant's power drew her back, her blue eyes transformed with fury, the white teeth champing with rage, the fair cheeks red with passion. The Count's eyes were blazing: the red light in them was lurid as if hell-fire blazed behind them. With a fierce sweep of his arm he hurled the woman from him and then motioned to the others, as though he were beating them back. In a voice which, though low and almost a whisper, seemed to cut through the air, he said:

"How dare you touch him, any of you. Beware how you meddle or you will have to deal with me!"

The fair girl, with a laugh of ribald coquetry, asked:

"Are we to have nothing this night?"

He nodded and kicked at a bag which he had thrown upon the floor, and which moved as though there were some living thing within it. One of the women jumped forward and opened it. There was a gasp and a low wail as of a half-smothered child. Then the women disappeared, and with them the dreadful bag. They seemed to fade into the rays of the moonlight and pass out through the window, for I could see outside the dim, shadowy forms for a moment before they faded away.

The next thing I knew it was broad daylight and there was the encouraging sound of voices and the movement of horses and wagons far below. There was no sign of Holmes in his room. Indeed I had slept far into the day. I made my toilet, using my old army mirror since there was not a looking glass to be seen.

I found Holmes in the dining hall where he had already breakfasted off cold cuts and cheeses. There was a pot of coffee warming on the hearth.

"There are servants after all," I said, "I hear them about in the courtyard."

"I think not," replied Holmes. "Certainly they are not part of the household. They are a band of Szgany, they speak in some form of Romany peculiar to themselves."

"You approached them?" I asked hopefully.

"I called down to them from the tower but they feigned not to hear me. They have leiter-wagons and were moving some odd looking boxes from somewhere out of sight. There is some digging going on. One can hear the muffled sound of mattock and spade."

"Boxes you say. What kind of boxes?"

Holmes smiled, evidently reading my thoughts.

"Great, square boxes, with handles of thick rope, clearly empty since the gypsies handled them with ease."

"Well," I said, "no doubt the Count will enlighten us."

"Perhaps," said Holmes, "when he returns. He left this note."

My friend handed me a paper on which was written in a spidery scrawl, "I am about your business and hope to have news for you this night." It was signed "Dracula."

The food looked appetising and I set to and ate heartily. I told my friend of my appalling nightmare and, to my surprise, he listened with interest since he was usually one to scoff at such things. I myself had already begun to put it down to the spicy foods we had been consuming.

Later we resumed our searches after again attempting to summon the attention of the gypsies. One or two appeared to look up at us but just then the "hetman" of the Szgany said something to them and they went about their business.

We returned to the rooms in the south wing and here after a lengthy search Holmes made an extraordinary discovery.

"Hulloa, look at this" he declared.

He had been examining shelves of ancient tomes and had found one that had been recently disturbed for the dust-laden cobwebs had shrivelled. He held the book open at the dry parchment of the fly-leaf. On it was a page of strange symbols.

"Some sort of hieroglyphics," I suggested. "Egyptian, perhaps?"

"No, Watson," replied. "It is the shorthand of Isaac Pitman. But look at these," he went on, pointing to the four corners of the inscriptions, "four crucifixes."

I was peering at them when he began to read:

"I was here held prisoner by Count Dracula in the Year of our Lord – "

"Astonishing," I began. "Blessed if I knew you could read shorthand." But Holmes ignored my interruption and continued:

" – in the Year of Our Lord eighteen ninety eight. I know not my fate at the hands of this Demon but entrust my soul to Almighty God, April 28th 1898. Janos Svbado."

"But that is only a few days ago," I said.

"Indeed," replied Holmes. "We may yet be in time."

We spent the remainder of the daylight hours trying to obtain access to the courtyard. We could hear the Szgany working below, there was the muffled thud of earth and the sound of heavy weights being dragged across stone floors. We succeeded in penetrating several of the rooms by working on the ancient locks, but none led to the courtyard. Most were bare save for rough pieces of furniture, dust-laden and rotten. As dusk approached we heard the gypsies moving away in their leiter-wagon and the castle fell to silence once more.

The evening wore on with no sight or sound of the Count. We decided to return to the tower and to keep watch by turns. The hours passed in eerie stillness except for the occasional barking of dogs far down in the valley. I was on watch when I thought I saw some movement below but a cloud drifted over the moon. I called to Holmes who was quickly by my side. As the cloud skirted the edge of the moon, there appeared a figure climbing swiftly towards the aperture from which we had seen the bat-like creature descend on the previous night. Slung at its side was a leather bag, like the one I had seen in my dream. The dark figure quickly disappeared through the aperture and for a time there was silence. Then there was a sharp wail, quickly suppressed, and again silence: a deep, awful silence which chilled me.

Before long, there was the sound of agonised cries from the courtyard below. We could dimly discern the figure of a peasant woman in great distress, tearing at her hair and sobbing piteously. She held her hands over her heart, as one distressed with running.

"Monster!" she cried out breathlessly. "Monster! Give me my child!"

Now we heard the voice of the Count calling in his harsh metallic whisper. His call was answered from far and wide by the howling of wolves. Before many minutes had passed, a pack of them poured through the gateway. The woman, who had continued to sob and scream over the beastly howling, was not now heard. She was out of our sight, beating with her bare hands on the great door when the wolves came.

Mercifully, they were quick about their bloody task. Before long they streamed away singly and disappeared into the night.

We resumed our watch, taking turns to sleep, since Holmes had determined that we must attempt our escape with the daylight. It was my friend's belief that the Count moved by night and slept by day. In the few remaining hours of darkness we would look out for him.

CHAPTER FIVE

When the sun rose cheerily my fear fell from me as if it had been a vapourous garment which dissolved in the warmth. Holmes had taken the last watch and was keen to make a start. We returned to the dining hall where the remains of the previous day's breakfast were untouched and the great fireplace was a mess of dead ashes. We pulled down the curtains and tapestries and with those and our bedding we began to make a long rope. Some of the fabrics were rotten with age but others were remarkably strong. Eventually we hauled our makeshift rope to the tower and were relieved to find that it appeared to fall level with the aperture below.

Once secured, Holmes made the first descent. The 'rope' strained and the knots stretched fearfully but it held. Holmes swung himself into the aperture and it was my turn. I made my way slowly and clumsily, my hands burning as they gripped the coarse fabrics.

Holmes was on hand to haul me in through the mullioned window. As I recovered my breath, he inspected the room. It was barely furnished with odd things which seemed never to have been used; the furniture was something in the same style as that in the south rooms, and was covered in dust. In an open chest was a heap of gold coins and chains and ornaments, some jewelled, and all old and stained.

Holmes spilled some of the coins onto the floor, sorting them briefly in a cloud of dust.

"None less than three hundred years old," he remarked. "Austrian, Hungarian, Greek, Turkish, clearly booty from the past."

There were two doors in the room, one was locked with no sign of a key but the other was ajar. Heavy and sagging it took our combined strength to haul it open. We went through and found that it led to a stone passage and circular steps which descended steeply.

We trod carefully for the stairs were dark, being only lit by loopholes in the heavy masonry. At the bottom was a dark, tunnel-like passage, through which came a deathly, sickly odour, the odour of old earth newly turned. As we moved along the smell grew closer and heavier until we found ourselves in a ruined chapel, which had evidently been used as a graveyard. The roof was broken, and in two places were steps leading to vaults, but the ground had recently been dug over and the earth placed in great wooden boxes.

"These are the boxes brought here by the Szgany," Holmes murmured.

"And the earth is used for some sort of packing." I said.

"I wonder," replied Holmes, seizing a stave and prodding the earth carefully in one of the boxes. After a few strokes he cast the stave aside and went down into the vaults. I followed him with some reluctance and stood at the entrance of one where the dim light struggled, although to do so was a dread to my very soul. Holmes used his torch, flicking the narrow beam to disclose fragments of old coffins and piles of dust. The next vault was much the same. Holmes moved into the third and I followed, a little bolder now. Even Holmes withdrew a little at the shock, as his torch revealed the Count lying in one of the great boxes on a pile of newly dug earth. His face was bloated, his eyes were open and stony, but without the glassiness of death. The cheeks had the warmth of life through all their pallor, and the lips were red and stained with blood.

Holmes bent over him. "No pulse, no breath, no beating of the heart. What say you, Watson?"

I went about my repulsive task.

"No sign of life, and yet –". I broke off at a terrifying cry from nearby.

"In the name of God, help me, help me!" cried a man's voice – weak, hoarse, exhausted. We moved out of the vault speedily, looking around in the dim light of the chapel.

"There!" cried Holmes, moving swiftly to another vault. Lying on the stone floor inside the vault, clutching at the iron gate was a young man, pale, unshaven, dishevelled, his clothes filthy, his hair grown long and matted with dirt. If this was Mina's young husband, he was unrecognisable from the young man I had met when he had studied in London.

Holmes grabbed at the bars of the gate but it was firmly locked. Looking around he saw a bunch of ancient keys on a hook a few feet away. The third fitted the lock.

The young may had dragged himself to his feet and as Holmes opened the gate he charged out like a wild man, screaming "He is here! The demon is here!"

Lurching, reeling, stumbling he ran into Dracula's vault. Holmes and I followed swiftly. By the light of Holmes's torch the young man saw a spade propped against the wall. He seized it and swung at the body of Count Dracula. As he did so the head appeared to turn and the eyes blazed. The sight seemed to paralyse the young man. The spade fell from his grip, striking a glancing blow which made a deep gash in the Count's forehead before it struck the flange of the lid, closing it in a cloud of dust. That last glimpse we had of the bloated face, bloodstained and fixed with a grin of malice would have held its own in the nethermost hell.

The young man screamed in terror and stumbled blindly from the vault. Holmes followed and was in time to catch him as he collapsed, breathing feverishly. I knelt over him, giving him a cursory examination. Physically, he appeared unharmed but I feared for his mental state.

Meanwhile Holmes searched the chapel and was examining the main doors when he called out to me:

"The Szgany are returning! I hear their wagons entering the courtyard!"

He ran back to me. "We must find a place to hide. Quick! The passage!"

We picked up the unconscious Janos and carried him into the passage. The Szgany were already at the doors, for we could hear them turning the lock. Holmes moved back into the shadowy chapel saying:

"It is better that I am free to observe."

I saw him run down the steps to close the gate to the vault where Janos had been held; then I lost sight of him as he disappeared into the gloom.

The Szgany set to work with a will, heaving and grunting as they dragged the many boxes out into the yard, evidently loading them onto their wagons. Once or twice, I caught sight of a few of them as I watched from behind the half-open door. They were a rough-looking, swarthy bunch but not work-shy. They sang snatches of some plaintive gypsy song as they went about their task, though they were silent and strangely subdued when they hauled the closed box from the Count's vault. Others backed away as the bearers passed them and the singing was not resumed.

It must have been an hour or more before they completed their task. It was as they were leaving that an angry commotion broke out, shouting at one another in their strange Romany tongue. Eventually they closed the doors and began to move off, still shouting angrily.

Suddenly Holmes reappeared.

"What was all that about?" I asked.

"Some fool mislaid the key," said Holmes with a brief smile, holding up the object of their dispute.

Janos shuddered fitfully as we carried him out of the foulness of the chapel into the chill air of the courtyard. Great thick clouds were drifting across the sky. There were signs of a coming storm in some lofty stratum of the air. We placed him in the shelter of a stable as dusty and cobwebbed as those awful chambers in the castle itself. Holmes would have pursued the Szgany and their strange cargo had it not been that our first duty was to the pitifully crazed young man.

It was decided that my friend should go in search of aid or some form of transportation while there was daylight to do so. He set off without delay.

As I looked out of the stable there came a cold shiver in the air and snow began to fall. I covered Janos with my coat but could do little to stem the tremors and moans as he shifted restlessly. Then the wind grew strong and blew with ever increasing force. I feared for Holmes in his lonely task. The air became icy cold. The snow was falling thickly and whirling around in such rapid eddies that I could hardly see across the courtyard. Every now and then the heavens were torn asunder by vivid lightning so that the clear lines of the hideous castle cut the sky.

By and by the storm seemed to be passing away; it now only came in fierce puffs or blasts. At such moments the weird sound of the wolf appeared to be echoed by many similar sounds around me. Then the ground shook as though thousands of horses thundered across it, and this time the storm bore on its icy wings, not snow but great hailstones which drummed on the ground.

Darker and darker grew the sky as approaching dusk merged with the lowering clouds.

Janos raved in his delirium of ghosts and demons, his body writhed as his fevered brain struggled with the awful imagery. I found a few rotten sacks to wrap around him but was helpless to do more to ease his suffering.

The howling wind shut out the sound of Holmes's approach. He had persuaded a reluctant peasant to come to our rescue with a lieter-waggon drawn by a pair of farm horses, twitching fretfully as they entered the environs of the castle. We were quickly away but it was a mile or more before the beasts settled.

We travelled for what seemed like hours through the forest, our path lined with snow-clad cypresses, until at length we reached an old monastery where the monks gave us shelter.

Our peasant friend was well rewarded and given a hot meal and a bed for the night. Meanwhile my first concern was for my niece's young husband. With the help of the monks he was put to bed on a simple cot piled with sheep-skins. We fed him a warm gruel and before long he fell asleep, his twitching and shivering becoming less and less. The monks elected to take turns watching over him and I was led to the refectory where supper had been prepared. I had not eaten since breakfast the day before. The warmth of the open fire and the roast turning on the spit was most welcoming. Holmes had waited for me and was engrossed in conversation with an aged monk, Brother Arminius, who knew much of the origins of the Draculas and was well read on the history of the revenants of Hungary and Moravia.

As we ate he spoke quietly of the Draculas. They were, he said, a great and noble race though now and again there were scions who were held by the coevals to have had dealings with the Evil One. Voivode Dracula, centuries ago, had won his name against the Turks. He was still spoken of as the cleverest and most cunning, as well as the bravest of the sons of "the land beyond the forest."

But in one ancient manuscript Voivode was spoken of as a "wampyr". There had been, said the monk, from the loins of this very man great men and good women, and their graves made sacred the earth where alone the vampire could dwell.

"For it is said," the old monk told us, "that not the least of its terrors is that the evil thing is rooted deep in all good; in soil barren of holy memories it cannot rest."

"The boxes," said Holmes, "we must find them."

When we had partaken the excellent supper, Brother Arminius led us into the library where he had at his finger tips several works on the subject of vampirism. Holmes' eyes lit up as he read some of the titles: "Magia Posthuma," "Phlegon de Mirabilibus," Dom Augustin Calmet's "Traits sur Les Apparitions Des Esprits et sur Les Vampyres, Ou Les Revanans."

"The lives of the Saints are full of resurrections of the dead," said Brother Arminius as my friend produced his magnifying glass, preparing to read far into the night. "But the resurrection involved in the belief of Vampirism is of a different and most evil kind."

I had long known of Holmes's amazing ability to shrug off fatigue. For myself, the excellent food and wine had appeased my need for everything save sleep. Brother Arminius led me to a simple cell furnished with a cot and a prayer stool.

I climbed into the cot clad in my undergarments, drew the fleecy goatskins over me and fell asleep with the flickering candle flame dancing on the stone walls of the tiny room.

When I awoke in the morning my first thought was for my young patient. I was pleased to find that he had slept peacefully for most of the night. The monks had bathed him and dressed him in a thick nightshirt and he had taken some nourishment. Now he lay on the cot, staring at the arched ceiling of the small infirmary. He seemed not to recognise me and a few words confirmed my belief that he was suffering from amnesia as well as from the shock of his ordeal.

At breakfast I discovered that Holmes had left with our peasant friend at first light and knew well that he had persuaded the poor wretch to take him on a search for the Szgany.

I spent much of the day in the infirmary. Janos veered from periods of tranquillity to periods of frenzied hysteria where he would scream and cringe against his imagined approach of some unspeakable horror. Only the mention of the name "Mina" appeared to reach his consciousness, giving him some peace of mind. "Yes, Mina," he would say quietly, "Mina."

"Your wife, Mina," I would say and he would answer wondrously, "Yes my wife ..." With that he would close his eyes and rest a little.

Holmes returned in the evening looking pale and exhausted. His efforts had been fruitless. Wherever they had gone the response had been the same.

No one would admit to having seen the gypsies and their mysterious load. Most of the peasants, apparently sensing the purpose of his inquiries, had crossed themselves and had held up their hands against him as if fending off evil spirits.

If our intervention had caused the Count to seek a new resting place, we were not likely to find it. I must say I wondered if this were not a good thing, after all, but I doubted if my friend would ever agree with such a view.

We remained at the monastery for several days, during which time Janos regained some strength but his amnesia remained as if he were fighting not to remember the awfulness that had gone before.

Holmes spent much of the time in conversation with Brother Arminius and with copious reading in the library. On our last night, after a simple but excellent repast, Holmes was in a mood to reflect on our recent experiences and on the wisdom of his learned friend, Brother Arminius.

"You know, Watson," he mused, "sometimes though we may reason well, we are too prejudiced. We do not let our eyes see nor our ears hear that which is outside our daily life."

I began to protest that I did not regard myself opposed to new thought but my friend went on:

"Do you not think that there are things which one cannot understand, and yet are; or that some people see things that others cannot? But there are things old and new which must not be contemplated by men's eyes because they know – or think they know – some things which other men have told them."

"Scientific knowledge," I began but this only warmed him to his subject.

"Ah, science," he interjected, "it is the fault of science that it wants to explain all, and if it cannot, then implies that there is nothing to explain. Do you believe in corporeal transference? Or in materialisation, astral bodies, thought reading, hypnotism?"

"Oh, well, Charcot has proved that pretty well," I said.

"Then you are satisfied as to that," he replied, "you accept hypnotism, as I do, but not, perhaps, thought-reading?"

He did not give me the time to assemble my reply.

"There are things done today in electrical science which would have been deemed unholy by the very men who discovered electricity – who would themselves not so long before have been burned as wizards. There are always mysteries in life. With all your knowledge of comparative anatomy, can you tell me why some men are brutes and others gentle? Can you tell me why other spiders die small and soon and one great spider lived for centuries in the tower of an old Spanish church and grew and grew until, on descending, it could drink the oil of all the church lamps? More to the point, why, in the Pampas, and elsewhere, there are bats that come in the night and open the veins of horses and cattle and suck them dry, or how in some islands of the Western seas there are bats that hang in the trees all day and at night when sailors sleep on deck because of the heat, they flit down upon them and drain their blood?"

"The Vampire Bat," I said.

"Indeed," he replied, "The Vampire Bat."

CHAPTER SIX

We left next day for Bistritz. A coach had been summoned and we were able to transport my young patient in reasonable comfort. He was still pale and thin and had little to say. Though in his mid-twenties his hair was streaked with grey. I feared my niece was in for a shock but I had written ahead to forewarn her and to assure her of his eventual recovery. We took the journey in stages in order that Janos should not be overstrained and when we arrived at Budapest, Dr Westenra met us with a private ambulance. Mina was waiting in front of the house when we arrived. Bravely she held back her tears.

Janos managed a wan smile, almost in tears himself, before they embraced. When Lucy appeared to greet her cousin, Janos flinched and drew back for a moment before recovering to return her greeting. I noticed that Holmes seemed alert to this curious exchange.

The young man was helped to his bed and Mina began the long vigil by his side which was to occupy her waking hours for some time to come. I warned her quietly not to tax him on recent events but to wait patiently for signs of his memory returning.

Rooms had again been prepared for us and Dr Westenra said he was looking forward to our stay. When we were alone after dinner that evening he asked us to tell him of our experiences in Transylvania. I must say I was surprised that as a man of science himself and a specialist in psychology and diseases of the mind, he was somewhat sceptical of our account. Perhaps Holmes was right in his argument that for some that which science could not explain implied that there was nothing to explain.

Dr Westenra was much more at home in his own field of the treatment of the insane and was positively enthusiastic in telling us of his current "pet" patient, a man whom he termed "zoophagous," a life-eating maniac. Holmes seized the opportunity to move away from the subject of Transylvania and before long had persuaded our host to take us on his nightly round of the neighbouring asylum, particularly if it was to include a sight of this patient, an otherwise scholarly man by the name of Renfield.

As we made our way through the gloom, ill-lit building sadly typical of such institutions, Dr Westenra told us more about his "pet".

"He has certain qualities that are very largely developed," he told us. "Selfishness, secrecy, and purpose. He seems to have settled on some scheme of his own, but what it is I do not yet know. For a time his hobby was catching flies until they became something of a nuisance. When I told him he must get rid of them he willingly agreed and promptly picked up a blowfly buzzing on the window ledge bloated with some carrion food. He held it exultingly for a few moments between finger and thumb and then put it in his mouth and ate it!"

Holmes listened impassively but I could scarcely stifle my disgust.

"Then there were the spiders," our host went on, much amused. "Several big fellows which he kept in a box, feeding them with his diminishing supply of flies. He next acquired a sparrow, feeding it, of course, from his supply of spiders. Before long he had quite a little colony of tame sparrows fed by the spiders, in turn fed by the flies, for he had begun to spread sugar for them on his window ledge once more. The other day when I visited him he ran to me, fawning and obsequious, and begged me a great favour. He wanted a kitten! 'A kitten,' he said, 'a nice little, sleek, playful kitten that I can play with and feed, and feed and feed ...' Since I did not want the sparrows to go the same way as the spiders and the flies I rejected his request. He became very angry and one could see at once that he is a homicidal maniac, most dangerous because he is a man of considerable strength as you will see."

We were in a corridor of locked rooms, much like cells, with peep-holes and feeding slots. As we walked along there was something of a commotion at the far end of the corridor where one of the attendants was summoning the assistance of a colleague.

"I think that is our friend Renfield causing some disturbance," said Dr Westenra before we reached the open door of the cell.

The man was crawling on the floor, hideously sick, having disgorged a whole mess of feathers. The attendant told Dr Westenra: "He's eaten his birds, just took them and ate them."

Whilst I was plainly revolted, Holmes was intrigued. Dr Westenra and his staff attended the man, inducing him to rid himself of the rest of his gruesome meal.

"A zoophagous maniac," Holmes murmured, "what he desires is to absorb as many lives as he can and has laid himself out to achieve it in a cumulative way. Had one the key to such a mind one would advance the knowledge of insanity to a pitch compared with Burdon-Sanderson's physiology or Ferrier's study of the human brain. Lunatics reason so well! I wonder at how many lives he values a man!"

At breakfast next morning Holmes and I listened with interest as Mina told of an incident during the night. Janos had settled down quite well and she, Mina, had at length thought it safe for her to try and get some sleep. But just as she was dropping off he began to tremble feverishly and to mutter "He is here! He is here!" At that the bedroom door opened and a shaft of moonlight spread across the floor. Lucy appeared in her long white nightdress, stopping in the doorway as if hesitating to proceed. Janos scrambled into a corner like a cowering animal crying out "No, no ..."

Mina had at once realised that Lucy was sleepwalking again, as she had done a number of times since we had been away. She went to her and turned her gently, guiding her back to her own room before running back to tend her husband.

"It is a very strange thing," she told us, "this sleepwalking, for as soon as her will is thwarted in any physical way, her intention, if there be any, disappears and she yields willingly."

Dr Westenra shook his head. "I am afraid the wedding next month is over exciting her," he said, "she is highly strung, poor child."

"Did your husband settle again?" Holmes enquired solicitously.

"Not until dawn," she replied. "I lit one of the lamps and held him in my arms, hoping that he would settle, but it was not until cock's crow that he finally relented and closed his eyes."

My friend was about to say something when Lucy entered the room, smiling radiantly and enquiring after us all like the perfect young hostess.

She then began to tell us in the most glowing terms of the virtues of her fiancé, Sandor, a young lieutenant in the Hussars.

When the meal was over I issued what I called "doctor's orders" to my niece that she should get some rest for I feared she might have several sleepless nights before Janos recovered. She told me that Eva, one of the family's servants was watching over him and that she would obey my orders.

The morning started out in a bright, Spring-like way, but as the day progressed dark clouds gathered and the air became quite chill. I was reminded of that awful day outside the castle and, indeed, a storm was on its way.

During the evening the stillness of the air became quite oppressive for a time. Then without warning the tempest broke. With a rapidity which seemed incredible the whole aspect of nature became convulsed. The wind roared like thunder and blew with tremendous force, literally bending the trees. To add to the dangers of the time a fog drifted over the city – white, wet clouds, which swept by in ghostly fashion, so dank and damp and cold that it needed but little effort of the imagination to think that the spirits of the dead were touching the living with clammy hands.

At times when the mist cleared one could glimpse the city below in the glare of lightning which now came think and fast, followed by peals of thunder which made the whole sky seem to tremble under the shock of the storm. We learned later that ships on the Danube were cast from their moorings, thick ropes snapped like string, their snaking whiplash hurling people into the raging torment of the river.

Holmes and I were at the window in the dining room looking out on the havoc of the storm when we discerned the wailing of a siren from the asylum and glimpsed figures in oilskins, carrying swinging lanterns as they made their way through the grounds. We saw Dr Westenra hurrying from the house and decided to offer such assistance as might be needed. We hauled on our greatcoats and hastened to the scene, impeded by the great gusts of wind that almost hurled us from our course.

One of the attendants shouted that Renfield, the madman, had escaped but they were on his trail.

Under cover of the thunder he had with manic strength ripped out the window frame and made off. Dr Westenra's deputy had been at his window watching the storm when he spotted the escapee.

We followed the others as they scrambled up the rising ground to a neighbouring estate. Bushes and tree branches lashed us as we made our way through a small copse. Beyond it stood a grey, forbidding mansion, shuttered and dark. On the far side of the house there was an old family chapel.

The jagged lightning seemed about to tear the building asunder. Renfield was pressed against the iron-bound oak door of the chapel, calling piteously, oblivious of the lashing wind and rain.

The attendants had him surrounded but were clearly hesitant to approach him. A couple of them were unfolding a straight waistcoat. Dr Westenra, elderly and somewhat frail though he was, moved towards the man. Holmes and I were close by him. We could hear Renfield shouting over the noise of the storm:

"I am here, Master, to do your bidding. I am Your slave and You will reward me, for I shall be faithful. Master, Master! Hear me! You will not pass me by in your distribution of good things …"

Just then he became aware of us and howled with rage. It was then or never. We all advanced. He seized Dr Westenra by the throat and would have shaken the life out of him had we not all charged upon the madman.

The doctor broke free, staggering and choking as we continued our struggle. It took six of us, four attendants and Holmes and I, to finally subdue him, whereupon he was jacketed and trussed and led away. He was immensely strong, more like a wild beast than a man. Even tightly constrained as he was he continued to struggle. I never saw a lunatic in such a paroxysm of rage before.

He turned back to the chapel, reeling wildly and shouting to his "Master".

"Remember me, Master, I am your slave," he cried.

We learned later that he had quietened somewhat and had been chained to the wall of the padded cell. They said his cries at times were awful but the silences that followed were more deadly since there was murder in his every turn and movement.

Meanwhile my friend and I accompanied Dr Westenra to his office at the asylum. We each had a warming brandy as we recovered from our exertions.

The storm finally abated and there was a strange quiet everywhere, broken only by the distant cries of poor Renfield and the occasional screams of other inmates disturbed either by the storm or by Renfield's outbursts. Dr Westenra elected to sleep in his office in case of any further alarms.

It was after midnight when we left him and trudged back over the sodden ground to the house. We were somewhat puzzled to find the door wide open though the hall was in darkness. As we were about to mount the stairs poor Mina came hurrying from her room carrying a lamp, a heavy wrap over her shoulders and another one on her arm.

"Oh, thank goodness, gentlemen," she whispered, "please help me. Poor Lucy is sleep-walking again."

We set out once more for the graveyard. There was a bright full moon with heavy black driving clouds, which threw the whole scene into a fleeting diorama of light and shade as they sailed across. For a time we could see nothing of Lucy. Then the silver light of the moon struck the bench far below where we had found her before. Sure enough there was a half-reclining figure in white. The coming of a cloud was too quick for us to see distinctly for shadow shut down on light almost immediately; but it seemed to me as though something dark stood behind the seat where the white figure shone and bent over it.

"There is someone with her!" I cried.

"Someone or something," answered Holmes, hurrying forward, leaping over the graves as he made his way toward the bench.

As we drew nearer we could distinguish more even through the spells of shadow. There was something, long and black, bending over the half-reclining figure.

Mina cried out in fright, "Lucy! Lucy!" and the figure raised its head, a white face and red gleaming eyes. A shudder went through my bones but we hurried on. Just then a heavy cloud obscured the moon. We reached her as the cloud passed. She lay back in the moonlight, her head against the topmost bar of the seat. She was quite alone and there was not a sign of any living thing about.

Lucy was still asleep. Her lips were parted and she was breathing not softly but in long, heavy gasps as though striving to fill her lungs at every breath. As we came near she put up her hand in her sleep to pull the collar of her nightdress close round her throat. After observing her for a moment Holmes moved swiftly among the gravestones, searching for the ominous figure we had observed.

I helped Mina raise the sleeping Lucy. Mina flung the shawl around her friend's shoulders and busied herself with a brooch to hold it in place. Then we led her slowly back up the steep hill.

We returned Lucy to her room and I left Mina to settle her into her bed, saying that I would look in on Janos in the next room. As I returned along the corridor I met Holmes coming from the stairs. He answered my questioning look with a shake of his head. When we entered Janos's room we found him huddled against the bed head in a state of evident terror. He stared right through us, his eyes unblinking. "He is here ... he is here ..." he muttered. "He is here ..."

It was important that Mina should be free to return to her husband but Holmes felt, and I concurred, that Lucy should be watched over for the remainder of the night. Mina wakened Eva, a faithful servant devoted to her young mistress.

With that we retired to our rooms but I doubted if my friend would seek the refuge of sleep. Indeed, when I took a last glance out of my window before climbing into bed I saw Holmes puffing on his pipe as he surveyed the graveyard below.

When I looked in on Lucy early next morning, Eva had been relieved by one of the younger servants. Apparently Lucy had been restless and had twice attempted to go out of the room. She was sleeping peacefully but I was alarmed to find tiny specks of blood on the collar of her nightdress and, on close examination, to detect two tiny wounds on her throat. The young maid had a ready explanation. Madame Mina had seen the marks which she must have caused when she fastened the shawl around Miss Lucy's neck. I wished I could accept that explanation.

I was telling Holmes of this development when Dr Westenra came into the breakfast room, looking pale and weary after his night at the asylum. By unspoken agreement we let Dr Westenra dictate the subject of our conversation. He waved the daily newspaper with its report of the storm.

"Havoc in the city last night," he reported, "ships broke from their moorings, churches struck by lightning, several poor souls swept into the Danube. Strangest of all, a barge fetched up on the bank with its captain lashed to the tiller, dead, and his crew a man and a boy both missing with signs of some awful struggle in the cabin, blood everywhere. It seems some fierce-looking dog leapt from the barge as that strange mist cleared."

Dr Westenra laid the newspaper aside and began to help himself to some breakfast.

"I'm afraid poor Lucy had a bad night," I told him.

"Again?" he asked, turning to me. "The walking in her sleep?"

"Yes," I told him. "We found her in the same spot. The seat in the graveyard."

"Poor child," he said. "I wonder if we should bring forward the wedding and confine it to a simple ceremony. The strain is clearly harming her."

Holmes was looking at the newspaper, his remarkable command of languages affording him the ability to read the article about the storm.

"Well, well," he murmured, "what have we here ... it seems the barge's cargo consisted of fifty large wooden boxes filled with ... I wonder if you could assist me with this word, Dr Westenra?" He pointed to the word and Dr Westenra readily interpreted:

"Mould," he said obligingly, "samples of earth, perhaps, for some agricultural purpose ..." He went on piling his plate with cold cuts and cheeses.

"Mould," repeated Holmes, fixing me with a gimlet stare.

Just then Mina entered the breakfast room. She too looked pale and tired. She told us that Janos had stayed awake again until first light but was now in a deep sleep. She had looked in on Lucy who had asked to be excused as she was not at all well.

Dr Westenra listened intently and then asked me if I would greatly oblige him by examining his daughter and, since I was already attending Janos, would I undertake to attend Lucy as well. I hesitated for a moment but Holmes answered for me.

"I'm sure my friend and colleague will be only too happy to be of service to you," he said.

"Of course," I said. "Only too happy, sir ..."

Dr Westenra thanked my profusely and continued with his meal. Holmes and I excused ourselves, saying that we would take a short stroll, and that then I would visit Lucy.

As we set off toward the graveyard Holmes cursed himself for a fool.

"Of course," he declared. "Of course they made for the river, there are a whole maze of tributaries that would lead to the Danube! And we were so bemused as to think that the Count sought a new resting place in that Godforsaken country while all the time he had planned for this. It was the very purpose of that wretched young man's journey into Transylvania!"

"What do you make of the report about the fierce-looking dog?" I asked, knowing the way my own thoughts were turning.

"Humph, you mentioned Grimpen Moor that night we journeyed to the castle. This time, I fear, there will be no such explanation as a phosphorus preparation on some oversized hound."

We were approaching the seat where we had found Lucy. Holmes took out his magnifying glass and began to examine the ground carefully, particularly the footprints in the wet soil behind the seat.

We were both thoroughly absorbed in the task when a cultured voice interrupted us.

"You are interested in old graveyards, gentlemen?" We were being addressed by an elderly man of scholarly appearance who was enjoying a pipe on a nearby seat.

"This is a peaceful spot with a fine view of the city," he said, "but I feel something of an interloper since I am not myself a believer in all this nonsense of an afterlife. Look at that stone under your feet. 'Sacred to the memory of Karoly Marias who died in the hope of a glorious resurrection.' The poor youth was a cripple from birth who blew his head off with a shotgun!"

Holmes had risen to his feet and pocketed his magnifying glass.

"A suicide, you say, sir. How very strange. In consecrated ground."

"His mother was a woman of influence. A compliant coroner returned a verdict of accidental death," the gentleman replied, knocking out his pipe and getting to his feet.

"Good day, gentlemen," he said walking away with a slow tread, "enjoy your researches".

"And this is a spot which Lucy seems drawn to," said Holmes quietly to me. "Do you think, perhaps, it is time you visited your new patient, Dr Watson?"

We set off for the house in thoughtful mood.

My friend waited below while I conducted by examination. Although she was of a pale and somewhat bloodless appearance I could not see the usual anaemic signs. In other physical matters I was quite satisfied with her condition. She complained of difficulty in breathing at times and of heavy, lethargic sleep with dreams which frightened her but regarding which she remembered nothing.

With her permission I asked Holmes to join us. He sat by her bedside, putting her at ease with a rare display of charm. He was most solicitous and was quite excessive in his praise of my medical skills. He would brook no "pooh poohing" from me.

At her request he even told her of some of our exploits together, none of which, he insisted, were as remarkable as my journals had made out. "He has a fearful taste for exaggeration," he said, wagging a finger at me in reproof. She was greatly intrigued by his re-telling of the affair of The Dancing Men. Holmes was far too modest in his account of how he broke that devilish code.

When she was happily relaxed, he asked her gently: "Tell me, last night, when you went to your favourite seat in the graveyard, what do you remember?"

The little colour there was in her cheeks drained away.

She said, "Why, I hardly remember anything. I suppose I was dreaming, but it seemed as if it was real. I ... I ... remember the dogs howling. There seemed to be so many of them, all howling at once. Then I have a vague memory of a tall, dark figure, with red eyes and something very sweet and very bitter all around me; and then I seemed to be sinking into deep green water, and there was a singing in my ears, as I have heard there is to drowning men; and then everything seemed passing away from me; my soul seemed to go out from my body and then, and then there was Mina putting a cloak around me and dear Dr Watson helping me return to the house ..."

She sank back onto the pillows, quite breathless. I told her that she had best be getting some rest and to be sure and take some nourishment. She promised she would and we withdrew.

CHAPTER SEVEN

We took a cab into the city, discussing Lucy on the way. It was obvious that she had not dreamed of the dark figure that we had seen with our own eyes. There was still a good deal of disruption in the centre of the city, a number of streets were closed and our driver was full of the events of the previous night. Certainly, he said, he knew where the barge had fetched up and would take us to the spot. But when we got there we discovered it had been refloated and taken elsewhere.

We dismissed the cab and proceeded on foot, inquiring the present whereabouts of the barge. Eventually we sighted a boat of the River Patrol but the young skipper, a somewhat pompous NCO, refused all information.

With his usual ingenuity Holmes resorted to a scheme that had often worked well for us in London. He recruited a bunch of young urchins, bribed them suitably with promises of double the amount for the right information and gave them our address. I thought it would be interesting to see how this Budapest version of the Baker Street Irregulars responded to the challenge. We called at a kiosk and obtained the latest newspapers and spent an hour or so at a boulevard cafe. Holmes left me for a time in order to despatch some communications from the Central Post Office. It was dusk before we set off for the Westenra home once more.

Our cab was passing below the graveyard when we got a glimpse of some curious activity within.

Several lanterns were flitting about and an ambulance wagon and other vehicles were drawn up at the gates. Holmes promptly ordered the cabbie to stop. He leapt out, leaving me to pay the man off, and hurried into the graveyard. I followed as quickly as I could and was in time to see by the light of the lanterns that a group of uniformed figures were examining the twisted body of a man lying at the foot of an awesome memorial of a guarding angel. The man's neck appeared to have been broken and his face was set in a terrifying grimace.

It was the scholarly man who had spoken to us that very day; the unbeliever who had questioned the propriety of his enjoyment of that peaceable place.

Just then a police dog was being led through the graveyard evidently as part of a search. It was when the animal neared the bench by the suicide's gravestone that it drew back, howling most dreadfully. It simply would not pass over the spot. The handler tugged at its lead but it backed away, writhing and yelping, baring its teeth in a vicious manner. The officer literally dragged it forward but it slipped its collar and raced away through the gravestones. It was then that we saw Lucy standing on the path below the house. She had a strange, faraway look on her face. As the dog's cries faded she turned, as if unseeing, and walked slowly back towards the house.

That evening Sandor Reviczky, Lucy's fiancé, came to dinner. Lucy seemed much improved if still a little pale. She was clearly happy in the presence of her young husband to be, chattering about the preparations for the ceremony and reception, all of which appeared to be planned on a grand scale.

Dr Westenra presided over a handsome table and my niece joined us, herself looking much rested, having left the good Eva to sit with Janos. It was a delightful family occasion. The servants were clearly excited by the coming event and the atmosphere was most pleasing. We enjoyed an excellent first course of the Hungarian fogas, said to be the most delicate freshwater fish in the world.

For myself I was rather relieved at the absence of paprika in the main dish; a boiled beef similar to the Viennese Tafelspitz, served with steamed potatoes and a mouth-watering creamed spinach. For dessert we had the famous Dobostorte, deceptively light for all its richness. The wines, from the Buda hills, were impeccable.

When the ladies withdrew we had the opportunity to learn something of young Sandor. Hungary is still a somewhat feudal society and Lucy's fiancé was a member of one of the great landowning families of the older aristocracy, enjoying a military career until such time as he would be required to take over the administration of considerable estates. A clean-cut, decent young man, he was clearly devoted to Lucy. His glorification of the hunting, shooting and riding life did not excite my friend but Holmes at all time maintained a deceptive display of polite interest.

After the rest of the household had retired to bed, Holmes and I took a stroll in the grounds, he enjoyed a pipe and I a good cigar.

We reviewed recent events and particularly the state of Lucy's health, the fact that despite there being no signs of her being anaemic, there had been considerable loss of blood. It was of paramount importance that she be protected, particularly during the night hours.

Her father's scepticism was a handicap to be overcome. When Holmes had introduced the subject of Renfield into our after-dinner conversation, Dr Westenra had dismissed the affair outside the old chapel as the typical religious paranoia of the insane.

Approaching the house after our turn around the grounds I noticed a slight movement at one of the upper windows. From its position I realised that it was most likely Lucy's bedroom.

"D' you see that, Holmes?" I said, pointing to the window.

"It is Lucy," he replied, "she appears to be leaning out of the open window."

"Getting some air, I expect," I said.

"On a chill night such as this?" said Holmes.

"Mmm, I think I had better go up," I said, moving away.

"Do that," said Holmes. "I say, there is a bird on the window sill. A bird ... or a bat!"

With that he quickly overtook me and we ran into the house.

Bursting into the room we were in time to see the bat, a huge thing, take off and flap away in a lazy fashion into the moonlight. Lucy turned, as if in trance, her stare unseeing.

"Lucy, my dear," I began.

With that she produced a strange smile: "Dr Watson ... Mr Holmes ..."

"We saw you from below," I said, speaking quietly in order not to alarm her. "You really should be in bed, the air is chill."

"Were you disturbed?" Holmes asked gently.

"I ... I ... was sleeping but I became so hot, I woke feeling the room was so oppressive and there was a strange tapping on the window. I fell asleep again and then ... you came in ..."

"But that creature on the window ledge -" I began.

"Creature?" she asked, "What creature?"

Holmes stepped forward, taking her hand.

"I think we should let the young lady get back to bed, don't you, doctor?"

I agreed. There was no point in alarming the poor child.

When she was settled again, I woke one of the maids and arranged for her to be in the adjoining room, Lucy's sitting room, throughout the rest of the night.

CHAPTER EIGHT

At breakfast next morning I was pleasantly surprised that Lucy should be joining us. She seemed tired but appeared to make a great effort to be cheerful and made no reference to the incident during the night. When we were alone in the morning room Holmes spoke quietly from behind the daily newspaper.

"Those tiny wounds," he said, "appear not to have healed."

"Mmm, they are still open," I replied, "and, if anything, larger than before."

"Do you notice the edges are faintly white?" he asked.

Just then there was a discreet tap at the door and a young housemaid entered to inform us that there was a visitor for Holmes at the kitchen door.

We followed the maid through to the rear of the house. Cook and the kitchen maids were much intrigued by my friend's business with the cheeky young scruff who had brought the required information.

We found the barge at a small floating dock on the Obuda quays, a district of Budapest quite provincial in its appearance, with crooked streets and peasant-baroque churches.

The police had evidently finished with the vessel. It swayed gently at its moorings, empty, alas, of its cargo.

We stepped aboard and looked around. Holmes went down into the hold and scooped a little earth into his hand, sniffing it carefully before brushing it off thoughtfully. I followed him to the tiny cabin which had evidently served as sleeping quarters. There were vivid bloodstains on the timbers; the bedding and other articles had presumably been removed by the police. Holmes saw something by the tiller and moved toward it. I, too, glimpsed the tiny reflection in the cold morning sunlight. He retrieved a small silver crucifix and a few beads from a broken rosary.

"The police have been less than thorough," he remarked as he pocketed the objects.

Our next task was to discover what had become of the barge's strange cargo. We inquired of several shipping agents in the area but to no avail. It was only after sampling the wares of a number of riverside taverns that we came across a local carter who admitted some knowledge of the boxes. He was well into his cups and not at all anxious to recall the event. Holmes and I took it in turns to ply him with his favourite tipple until he loosened his tongue. It seemed he had been approached by a tall gentleman of sickly appearance who had offered to pay him generously to remove and deliver the boxes the previous night.

He had attempted to put the job off until daylight but the man had been most insistent and had, in fact, doubled the price. He and his labourer had loaded the boxes onto his wagon and driven through the night to a deserted house where the tall gentleman had awaited them. Our informant became quite fearful when he spoke of the house, it being dusty and cobwebbed and overrun with rats.

The work had taken almost until the dawn and the gentleman had become quite agitated at their slowness, even picking up some of the boxes single-handed whereas they had sweated a good deal, even with two pairs of hands.

At length he gave us the address and we were able to take our leave.

We summoned a cab and set off immediately. I was astonished to discover that it was the very house Renfield, the lunatic, had escaped to on the night of the storm. Holmes made little of it, being far more intent upon gaining entry but the place was securely barred and bolted.

Forestalled, Holmes raised his stick and pointed in the direction of the asylum.

"I think it might be appropriate to pay a visit to Dr Westenra and, perhaps, his patient, Renfield."

I agreed and we went to the gates where a somewhat sullen gatekeeper doubted it would be convenient. Apparently there had been a disturbance in the close confinement wing. However he sent a message to Dr Westenra and was clearly surprised when an attendant came to collect us.

Dr Westenra was dressing a wrist wound on one of his male nurses when we entered his office.

"Renfield, I am afraid," he said, indicating to the wound. "He seemed to have settled down and we released him from the padded cell and returned him to his room. Last night he resumed his mutterings about The Master but was otherwise peaceable enough. During the day he began encouraging the flies again with a sprinkling of sugar on the window ledge in his room. It seemed harmless enough. This evening Anton here was giving him a controlled dose of an opiate when Renfield seized his wrist and bit him. Anton called for assistance and Renfield dropped to his knees licking up the blood dripping from the wound, uttering some nonsense about 'The blood is the life ...' I fear I will have to confine him again."

"A pity," said Holmes, to my surprise, "it would be most interesting to discover whether he is still interested in the old house on the adjoining property."

"Why do you say that?" asked Dr Westenra, clearly intrigued.

Holmes hesitated, looking in the direction of the male nurse who was flexing his hand after the doctor's ministrations.

"That should heal well enough, Anton," the doctor hold him. "The wound is clean and thoroughly disinfected." He gave the man a dismissive nod. Anton withdrew after thanking the doctor and bowing curtly to Holmes and I.

"Mr Holmes," Dr Westenra began, "much as I am fascinated by your reputation, I find it difficult to fathom your reasoning. Renfield is a sad case, a religions maniac, with some morbid fascination about eternal life. His interest, whether with spiders and flies or with The Master, whoever that is, is a pathetic aberration."

Holmes nodded pleasantly. "Quite so," he said, "but you may be interested to know that the cargo – a quantity of large wooden boxes of 'mould' I think you said, from that barge that ran aground in the storm, was delivered during the night to that otherwise deserted house. Curious, would you not say?" Westenra's face had darkened as he listened to Holmes.

"Most curious, I must agree," he said.

"Might I suggest something?" Holmes asked.

"But of course," the doctor answered.

"Why not let Renfield escape?" suggested Holmes.

Dr Westenra pushed back his chair.

"Let him escape?" he repeated with astonishment. "The man is a dangerous lunatic!"

"A 'controlled' escape," replied Holmes, beaming in a most reasonable manner.

Westenra sat forward in his chair.

"Controlled? How controlled?" he asked.

"A small display of carelessness on the part of your staff. The lunatic has a criminal brain, and criminals tend to think on the lines of the gullibility of others. It is their stock in trade. To the criminal we are all fools ..."

"Mmm," mused the doctor, "that business of the boxes is most odd ..."

Holmes smiled. He knew he had baited the hook.

My friend's plan was that we should all three visit the patient. Lull him and mollify him and, by an act of negligence, afford him the opportunity to escape. He was sitting on his bed staring at the floor when the door was unlocked and we entered the simple, barely furnished room.

He looked up and smiled:

"Ah, gentlemen, how good of you to come," he said. "I hope that our confrontation in the storm brought you no harm."

"None whatever," replied Holmes affably.

Renfield turned to Dr Westenra:

"So, you have come to remonstrate. I bit the hand that fed me! Why not, when your 'treatment' is an attempt to dull my faculties and turn me into a vegetable?"

"I hear you have resumed your activities as a fly-catcher," Dr Westenra replied, "would you like some more sugar for them?"

Renfield laughed: "No, thank you. Flies are poor things, after all. I don't want their souls buzzing around me."

"Then what about the spiders?," Dr Westenra asked.

"Blow spiders," Renfield replied with a flash of anger, "What's the use of spiders? There isn't anything in them to eat or – ". He stopped suddenly.

"- or drink?" Holmes offered quietly.

Renfield eyed Holmes with increasing suspicion before he answered:

"I don't take any stock at all in such matters. Of 'Rats and mice and such small deer,' as Shakespeare has it. 'Chicken feed of the larder' they might be called. I'm past all that sort of nonsense. You might as well ask a man to eat molecules with a pair of chopsticks as to try to interest me in the lesser carnivora, when I know what is before me."

"And what is that?" asked Holmes.

Renfield laughed in what became a somewhat idiotic giggle.

"You want bigger things to get your teeth into?" said Dr Westenra, as if talking to a child. "How would you like to breakfast on elephant? I wonder what an elephant's soul is like."

Renfield seemed to become despondent:

"I don't want an elephant's soul. I don't want any soul at all!"

Suddenly he jumped to his feet, with his eyes blazing and all the signs of intense cerebral excitement.

"To hell with you and your souls!" he shouted. "Why do you plague me about souls? Haven't I enough to worry and pain and distract me already without thinking of souls?"

In the next instant he became calm and said apologetically:

"Forgive me, Dr Westenra, I forgot myself. I am so worried in my mind that I am apt to be irritable. If you only knew the problem I have to face and that I am working out, you would pity and tolerate and pardon me."

He looked at Holmes and I as if we had some influence in the matter.

"Pray do not put me in a straight-waistcoat. I want to think, and I cannot think freely when my body is confined."

"We shall see," said Dr Westenra.

"You are most kind, Dr Westenra. You look tired, sir, if I may say so. I expect you have much to do, with your daughter's wedding approaching."

"You know of that?" asked Holmes.

Renfield looked at him again, his eyes narrowing for a moment:

"You will understand, gentlemen, that when a man is loved and honoured as our host is, everything regarding him is of interest to our little community. Dr Westenra is loved not only by his household and his friends, but even by his patients, who, being some of them hardly in mental equilibrium, are apt to distort causes and effects. Since I myself have been an inmate of a lunatic asylum, I cannot but notice that the sophistic tendencies of some of its inmates lean toward the errors of *non causae* and *ignoratio elenchi.*"

"You have a nice understanding of elemental philosophy," Holmes complimented him.

Renfield shrugged, barely concealing his contempt.

"If, gentleman, life is a positive and perpetual entity, then, as the Scriptures have it, 'The Blood is

The Life.' Though, indeed, the vendor of a certain nostrum has vulgarised the truism to the very point of contempt."

He turned to Dr Westenra with an ingratiating smile:

"You really should give me my discharge, doctor. It would be better for you and yours ..."

Dr Westenra looked at Holmes and I.

"I think we should leave our friend for the moment, gentlemen. I must consult with my deputy. Goodnight, Mr Renfield."

Renfield flopped onto his bed and turned away, saying resignedly:

"Goodnight, gentlemen."

We went out into the corridor. Dr Westenra left the door ajar as he called to an attendant:

"Ask Dr Lukacs to join me, Petrof."

We went down the corridor and before long heard the scurrying feet of Renfield travelling in the opposite direction.

Predictably, he made straight for the old chapel. Attendants were already posted and there was no risk of him getting away in any other direction. We made our way by a circuitous route which enabled Holmes to get nearest to him with myself close by. The man was on his knees in a prayer-like attitude:

"Master, Master!" he was saying in an urgent whisper, "oh how I rejoiced to hear your arrival at dead of night. I shall be with you. They shall not frustrate me. They shall not rob me of my joy. They shall not murder me by inches. You will save me!"

Just then there was a flapping sound above.

Renfield looked up and turned to watch the dark silhouette of a large bat flying away toward the city.

With that he saw his guardians standing in the gaunt shadows of the cedar trees.

"You need not tie me," he said with a smile, "I shall go quietly."

It was when he saw Holmes that his anger surged up once more:

"You, sir, will pay dearly for your meddling ..."

With that he walked forward, arms outstretched, into the hands of the attendants.

"Good night, Mr Renfield," said Holmes before turning to look once more at the old house, shuttered and silent.

Dr Westenra had stayed deep in the trees and was more interested in the fact that his patient had surrendered meekly than with what he called "these strange ramblings about his Master." Strangely my colleague elected not to argue the point.

CHAPTER NINE

We had a late supper at the house. Lucy and Mina had already retired and the doctor had remained at the asylum. I looked in on Lucy, who was already sleeping, and made sure that one of the maids was sitting up with her. It was the faithful Eva's turn and she was to be relieved during the night.

With that we too prepared to retire but Holmes took to bed with him some ancient tome his friend Brother Arminius had given to him. When I suggested he might be better off getting a good night's sleep, he tapped the leather-bound volume with his finger and said:

"The old physicians took account of things their successors do not. We must keep an open mind when we are dealing with the unknown."

Next morning I awoke at first light with an uneasy feeling that all was not well. I refreshed myself, pulled on some clothes and went along to Lucy's room. I tapped gently and as there was no answer I went in. Lucy lay quite still in the shadowy reaches of the room. The first thing I notice was that the curtains were flapping gently and the window was wide open. Before I went to her bedside I glanced into the adjourning sitting room. A young maid was sprawled on a settee, her mouth open, fast asleep. I drew back the curtains to let the light flood into the room. I crossed over to Lucy and looked down upon her. I was appalled. She was ghastly, chalky pale; the red seemed to have gone even from her lips and gums, and the bones of her face stood out prominently; her breathing was painful to see or hear.

I went to the door of the sitting room and shouted at the sleeping maid:

"Get Dr Westenra at once!" I cried. "At once, do you hear me?"

The girl shot up, eyes wide open now. She stumbled to her feet, straightened her dress and curtsied before she hurried away saying, "Yes, sir! Yes, sir!"

I moved out into the hall, made for Holmes's room, rapping on the door and calling:

"Holmes! Holmes! Come at once!"

I hurried back to Lucy. She stared up at me, unable to speak.

Holmes ran into the room gathering his robe about him.

"What is it?" he asked anxiously.

I let him look at her before pulling him aide:

"She will die for sheer want of blood to keep the heart's action as it should be!"

"My God, this is dreadful," he replied.

"There is no time to be lost," I told him, "there must be a transfusion of blood at once."

"I will willingly give blood," he said.

At that Dr Westenra came in. It took but a few words to acquaint him with the situation. He hurried off to get his bag.

Holmes glanced over at the open window.

"Was it open?" he asked.

"Yes," I said with a sigh.

"And the maid asleep," he said without waiting for a reply.

Just then there was the sound of horse's hooves on the gravel below. I looked out to see young Sandor evidently on morning exercise form the barracks of the Royal Palace. At first it seemed an unfortunate time to call but I reflected that his young blood might never be put to a better purpose.

Holmes went down at once to prepare him for the shock. He told me later that the young man took it well and volunteered even before Holmes suggested that he might give his blood.

Poor Westenra was badly shaken, I could see his hands trembling as he unfolded his instruments. He seemed deeply grateful when I took over from him. He was almost in tears when he looked down on his daughter. Young Sandor came in with Holmes, nodded briefly and silently to Dr Westenra and I, as we began our task. Lucy looked up at us, she was simply too weak to say anything. As the transfusion went on something like life seemed to come back to poor Lucy's cheeks and through Sandor's growing pallor the joy of his face seemed absolutely to shine. After a time I began to be a little concerned, for the loss of blood was telling on Sandor, strapping young fellow that he was. It gave me some idea of what a terrible strain Lucy's system must have undergone that what had weakened him had only partially restored her.

I terminated the transfusion and dressed his wound, sending him off for a glass of port wine and a good, hearty breakfast.

Lucy managed to smile at him before she closed her eyes and fell into a gentle sleep, her breathing stronger and more even now.

When we eventually joined the young officer in the breakfast room he sheepishly acquiesced to another glass of port which Dr Westenra insisted on pouring for him. Otherwise it was a rather solemn repast. When Mina learned what had happened she wanted to go at once to her friend but Holmes detained her:

"How is your husband?" he asked, "Did he sleep well?"

Mina, distraught, shook her head:

"I'm afraid not. He seemed to be in the midst of a terrible nightmare but he could not struggle to the surface. I tried to wake him but he tossed and turned and rambled on in a terrible anguish ..."

Sandor was persuaded to stay at the house and rest. A message was sent to the barracks and his horse was stabled.

Dr Westenra was a changed man, his face was ashen and his hands shook.

"That poor child," he said with a sob in his voice, "but for you, gentlemen, I would have lost her. Even now I cannot accept it, vampires, demons, I feel as if I am a candidate for my own asylum."

He looked at us pleadingly:

"What are we to do?"

"We must protect her every minute of the day and night," Holmes told him. "She must not be left alone for a moment."

It was agreed that the men should take turns throughout the hours of darkness and that Mina and the servants should keep watch during the day.

Dr Westenra was summoned to the asylum as there had been some unrest among the inmates during the night, evidently led by the curious keening of the wretched Renfield. Before the doctor left, Holmes asked him for an introduction to the National Library, which he gladly arranged.

When he had gone, Holmes told me that he might have discovered a nostrum which, he feared, would not be acceptable to modern science. His lengthy reading of the previous night required further confirmation.

With that he set off for the city. I looked in on Lucy from time to time. She slept peacefully into the early afternoon. She awoke dreamy and enfeebled but reluctant to eat. I managed to persuade her to take a little warm broth.

When Holmes returned in the evening he was carrying a crudely packaged parcel from the market.

"What on earth is that?" I asked.

"Flowers," he said with a brief smile. "Flowers for your patient."

"It looks an odd sort of bouquet to me," I answered.

Holmes had removed his hat and coat and started for the stairs.

"Shall we go up, doctor? He asked pleasantly.

I had little alternative but to follow him.

Holmes made an amusing mystery of the parcel and Lucy was suitably intrigued.

"These are for you, Miss Lucy," he said, holding up a great bunch of white flowers. "Not for decoration but as a medicine."

Lucy pulled a face.

"Not as a decoction or in a nauseous form," he told her, "but as protection, shall we say, against a strange ... infection."

Holmes worked with his usual brisk efficiency. "Some of it we will place by your window and some we will make into a garland around your neck."

"But it is garlic, Mr Holmes," said Lucy, "common garlic."

Holmes smiled and continued with his work.

"It smells like the waters of Lethe," he told her, "or of that fountain of youth that the Conquistadores sought for in the Floridas."

Lucy would have protested to me but I told her, in my best bedside manner, that it was for her own good, whereupon she submitted gracefully and watched us as we went about our task. Holmes fastened the window securely and I copied his actions as he rubbed a handful of the flowers into the sashes as though to ensure that every whiff of air that might get in would be laden with the garlic smell. Then we rubbed all over the jamb of the door, above, below and at the sides and around the fireplace in the same way.

When Holmes was ready to place the garland around her neck, Lucy seemed to have tired of all the attention and was beginning to slumber.

"You must not remove this," Holmes told her quietly.

She nodded her head, as if to understand.

Since this was evidently Holmes's "strange nostrum" I had made no protest but waited until later to observe that his remedy, if it were such, was not to be found in any pharmacopoeia I had ever heard of.

Dr Westenra took the first watch. He shook his head when he saw the garlic, his knowledge of his country's folklore precluded any need of an explanation. When I relieved him at midnight he reported that Lucy was sleeping peacefully though she had stirred restlessly at a strange tapping at the window. He had looked out into the night but there was nothing to be seen.

My watch passed peacefully. Holmes relieved me at four am, clean shaven and spruce. In the morning he too reported an uneventful spell. Lucy was much recovered and chatted happily with Sandor and Mina. She made light of her garland, saying there was "peace in its smell."

That night, being sufficiently recovered, Sandor insisted upon taking the first watch, to be relieved by Dr Westenra at midnight. His supper was sent up to him together with a goulash for Lucy, who was still reluctant to eat. At least the presence of her fiancé was an encouragement though I noted that she ate very little.

Westenra's appalling cry alerted us to a fresh crisis. On going to relieve Sandor he found him prostrate, the window open and Lucy, the garland cast aside, seemingly in a swoon. Dr Westenra was bent over her anxiously:

"It is not too late," he said as we rushed into the room, "Her heart beats, though feebly, but all our work is undone!"

Holmes took in the situation at a glance and crossed to Sandor who appeared to be in a heavy stupor.

"Laudanum!" he declared, sniffing the wine glass on the discarded supper tray.

"My God!" said Dr Westenra, "someone must have tampered with my medicines."

"We must act quickly," I warned. With that Holmes removed his smoking jacket and proceeded to roll up his sleeve.

Dr Westenra was almost in tears. "How can I thank you?" he asked hopelessly.

"Get the instruments," Holmes told him with a reassuring smile.

Dr Westenra hurried back with his bag and I took over once more, with him in attendance. "I think you should prepare an injection of morphia," I told him. He readily concurred, knowing that if, with growing strength, she awoke the shock might be too much for her.

Holmes withstood the loss of blood with typical stoicism and, at length, the transfusion was sufficient. Though paler than usual, he stood up and rolled down his shirt sleeve. "I think a night-cap might be in order," he said with a wan smile. "Will you join me, Dr Watson." I agreed readily, if only to attend on him and make sure that he rested.

I would have relieved Dr Westenra earlier but he would not hear of it. At length Holmes agreed to rest and I walked the grounds in the early hours. When the clock struck four I went up to Lucy's room. Her father was grey with fatigue yet reluctant to turn in. With the coming of dawn, Lucy stirred a little until she opened her eyes and summoned a weak smile.

"Sleep," I said, returning her smile, but she shook her head.

"No, no" she said, "I am afraid."

"There is no need to be," I told her, "you are in good hands."

"But this terrible weakness comes to me in my sleep until I dread the very thought."

"Sshh," I said, "it is daylight. You have nothing to fear." She closed her eyes and after a time she began to breathe evenly and eventually slept far into the morning.

Holmes showed little sign of his exhausting experience although he did eat an unusually hearty breakfast. Sandor was distraught at what he saw as his failure to take care of Lucy. Holmes would have none of it.

"You were drugged," he said bluntly.

"But who would do such a thing?" the young man asked in great distress.

"Strange forces are at work," Holmes told him, "and we must combat them. Will you join forces with us whatever the cost – for Lucy's sake?"

Sandor ran his hand through his hair.

"Need you ask me, sir?" he said quietly.

No, I doubt that I do," said Holmes, "but we are up against a formidable adversary, the like of which I have never known before."

"I am at your service," said the young officer, pale and unshaven.

CHAPTER TEN

Lucy remained stable throughout the day and we prepared carefully for our nightly vigil, replacing the garlic with a fresh supply. In the late afternoon Holmes and I took a stroll, trespassing unobserved in the grounds of the old house. The watery sun was sinking and the air grew quite chill as we examined the heavy doors and shuttered windows. It was only when we decided to return that we became aware of the vapourous mist which had gathered and which now swirled around us like a London fog.

In a matter of seconds we were unsighted. Holmes called to me to stay close but I had lost him completely. Had it not been for the sudden wail of the siren we might have stumbled around in the murk for an age but at least the siren acted as a guide. Holmes reached the wall first and renewed his calls to me. I pushed my way blindly through low hanging branches until I, too, found the wall. We joined up and edged our way to the gatehouse. Here the overhead gas lights made a poor impression in the mist but we were able to find our way into the main building.

We were met by a fearful commotion. The inmates in their confinements were setting up a terrible din. Attendants were running to and fro but we were unhindered as we made our way to Renfield's section.

Dr Lukacs and three attendants emerged from Renfield's room struggling with the straight-jacketed lunatic. They were dragging him toward the padded cell when he saw us.

Wild-eyed and raging he shouted:

"I begged him to release me! I warned him as I warned you! I did my Master's bidding!"

He was thrust into the cell and his cries were muffled by the deadening softness of that awful place.

By now we had reached Renfield's cell. Dr Westenra lay on the floor, his face contorted in the rictus of sudden death.

Dr Lukacs shook his head sadly. "His heart. He knew he was at risk but his work was his life. Renfield asked to see him just as he was leaving. The man seemed calm enough and there was an attendant present. Suddenly the patient flew into a rage and leapt at the doctor. He died instantly."

Somewhere a bell tolled the hour.

Holmes turned to me, his ascetic face haggard and drawn:

"Lucy!" he said, "we must return at once!"

We hurried out of the building to be confronted by the swirling mist, even denser now that night had fallen.

"Sandor is at the barracks," said Holmes, "the child is unguarded!"

He entered the gatehouse and commandeered a lantern before the duty guard could prevent him. We set out in the direction of the house, managing to discern a route of sorts from the fencing and the position of the trees.

Though the house was well-lit when we came upon it we saw nothing until we were within a few feet of the front door.

Holmes set the lantern aside and bounded up the stairs, with myself close on his heels.

Mina ran out onto the landing:

"Oh, Uncle John, Mr Holmes!" she cried, "Lucy is unconscious! There was a fearful crash and the sound of breaking glass. I ran to her room but the door would not open – it was if it were held by a raging wind!"

The door was wide open now and we ran in to find a mess of broken glass all over the floor and the window frame broken and twisted. Eva was kneeling over a young housemaid, treating her with smelling salts. Lucy lay on the rumpled bed, her breathing shallow, her face gaunt, blood spattered around those awful pin-pricks on her throat, all puckered and white.

"Look!" said Holmes. Lucy's lips were drawn back. Her teeth seemed to be longer and more pointed, like those of the Count.

"My God!" I said, "It is too late ..."

"Not while she lives," he replied. "She can be his only in death ..."

The maid was stirring now. She screamed as she recovered consciousness:

"The Wolf!" she cried. "The wolf burst through the window!"

She began to cry helplessly as Eva guided her out of the room.

"If there is the slightest chance," said Holmes. He glanced at Mina and I knew what he was thinking. There was a rustling sound by the window. We all turned. The mist had cleared and the stars were out. The branch of a tree brushed the window ledge.

I looked at my niece. "Mina," I said, "the only hope for Lucy is an immediate transfusion. Will you give blood?"

"Of course," she replied without a moment's hesitation. I fetched Dr Westenra's instruments and this time Holmes assisted me.

Lucy regained some of her colour but she was desperately enfeebled. When we had done we told Mina of Dr Westenra's death and it was agreed that Lucy should not be told, lest the shock be too much for her. Mina was anxious to return to her husband but was content that Eva was watching over him. Poor Janos was in a deep sleep, twitching and mumbling as if suffering another of his awful nightmares.

Sandor arrived just as we were preparing to move Lucy to another room. He gathered her up into his arms and carried her gently, her head resting against his shoulder.

We sat with her throughout the night but I feared for her survival. The trauma had been so great. Holmes prepared the room with garlic and once more placed a fresh garland around her neck. Lucy's breathing was stentorous, her face was at its worst, as white as the lawn of her pillow. When her lips were drawn back, her canine teeth, in particular, seemed longer and sharper.

Presently she moved uneasily. There was a dull flapping or buffeting at the window. Holmes crossed swiftly and ran up the blind. There was a full moonlight and a great bat wheeled and struck the window with its wings. Holmes lowered the blind grimly and returned to the bedside where Lucy had torn the garlic flowers from her throat. Holmes replaced them with care.

At length she opened her eyes and stared at us each in turn. Now she clutched the flowers to her throat but when, after a few moments, she sank into a shallow sleep she seemed to want to tear them away again. Holmes restrained her gently. In the long hours that passed she had many spells of sleeping and waking. Each time she would clutch the flowers to her on waking and then, in her sleep, attempt to push them away.

I must confess I was dozing when Holmes tapped me lightly on the shoulder. When I opened my eyes he pointed to her throat. The pin-prick wounds had entirely disappeared. I nodded in silent agreement. It was obvious that she was fading away.

"It will not be long now," I told my friend.

Holmes wakened Sandor who was slumped in a chair by the window. He knew at once that the end was near. He crossed himself and forced a brave smile.

"Summon all your fortitude," Holmes told him quietly.

As we returned to her bedside, Lucy awakened.

She looked up at her fiancé, a dream-like expression on her face.

"Sandor, my love," she whispered.

He bent down to kiss her but Holmes stayed him with his hand.

"No, not yet. Hold her hand, it will comfort her more."

The young man did as he was told. Gradually her eyes closed and she slept once more. For a time her breast heaved softly and her breath came and went like a tired child's. And then insensibly there came a strange transformation in her. The breathing became heavy, the mouth opened and the pale gums, drawn back, made the teeth look longer and sharper than ever. In a sort of half-sleeping, half-waking, vague, unconscious way she opened her eyes, which were now dull and hard at once.

She spoke in a soft, voluptuous voice, such as I had never heard from her lips:

"Sandor, oh, my love, come to me! Kiss me!"

The young man bent forward eagerly but at that moment, Holmes, who like me, had been startled by her voice, held him back. "Not for your life!" he said. "Not for your living soul and hers!"

Sandor stared at him, aghast. Holmes pointed to Lucy. A spasm of rage contorted her features most evilly. Her sharp teeth clamped together in an awful grimace. Then her eyes closed and she breathed heavily for a few seconds until, suddenly, her breathing ceased.

"It is all over," I said.

"It has only just begun," said Holmes.

The young man, uncomprehending, sank to his knees by her bedside, sobbing inconsolably.

Holmes was staring at the poor girl. He drew a quick hiss of breath and I followed his gaze.

Some change had come over her body. Death had given back part of her beauty, for her brow and cheeks had recovered some of their flowing lines, even the lips had lost their deadly pallor. It was as if the blood, no longer needed for the working of the heart, had gone to make the harshness of death as little rude as might be.

CHAPTER ELEVEN

Early that morning the undertakers arrived. They had much of the traditional suavity, unctuously reverential. The woman who performed the last offices for the dead said to me:

"She makes a very beautiful corpse, sir. It is a privilege to attend upon her."

It was arranged that Lucy and her father should be buried two days hence at the family vault in the city cemetery. Sandor helped with many of the arrangements as there were no near relatives. There was a great deal of weeping and grieving among the servants, some of whom had served the family since Lucy was an infant.

Presently Holmes asked to see the young maid who had been with Lucy the previous evening.

The maid, a stoutish country girl with apple cheeks, was greatly distressed but Holmes coaxed the story out of her with his usual charming, if steely, insistence.

She told him that Lucy had been resting quietly when they heard a strange howling outside, like a dog, only fiercer and deeper. The maid had lifted the blind and looked out but the mist swirled so thickly that she could not see the ground. Then she noticed that the gas lights burned blue and dim and that the air outside the window seemed full of specks like fireflies floating and circling. The howling grew fiercer and she backed away from the window and ran to Lucy who reached up and clasped her.

Just then the window shattered and the blind blew back with a great rush of wind. In the broken window frame there was the head of a great gaunt grey wolf. The dancing flecks floated around it and into the room.

At that the maid fell in a faint, dragging the garland from Lucy's throat as she collapsed. She remembered nothing more until the salts revived her.

The poor girl sobbed bitterly as she finished her tale. Like the others she had been devoted to Lucy.

Holmes thanked her and she curtsied, summoning a sad smile.

"It's all in the paper," she said as she made for the door.

"What is?" Holmes asked sharply.

"About the wolf," she said, looking at him as if he were mad.

"Thank you," he said, recovering, "of course."

When the girl had gone he crossed to the table where the newspapers were arranged. He took up a copy of the Budapesti Naplo and found the story on the front page.

"Listen to this, Watson," he said as he read the article:

"Berserker, a grey wolf from the Banat Mountains of Transylvania, escaped yesterday afternoon from the City Zoo. Shortly after feeding time for the wolves, jackals and hyenas, the normally placid Berserker grew restless and began to prowl the cage, hurling himself against the bars in a strange frenzy. The Keeper was tending a young puma down with an ailment when he heard the other wolves set up an intense howling and he became aware of a crashing and splintering. Hurrying back to the wolves' section he found Berserker's cage broken and twisted. The animal had disappeared."

"I'll be blessed," I said.

"I think a visit to the zoo is called for, don't you?" said Holmes, expectantly.

With that he hurried out and I followed him, glad, at any rate, to be away from the house of mourning, if only for a time.

The Superintendent of the Zoo was most impressed upon receiving a visit from Holmes and I. That he knew of Holmes's reputation was of some gratification to me. The gentleman insisted on accompanying us on our visit to the wolves' enclosure where the Keeper could answer our questions. The Superintendent looked like a high government official in his top hat and black cloak over a sober suit. The Keeper, a ruddy-faced man with the wolfish look of one of his charges, seemed not to recognise his superior at first.

When Holmes led him over the events of the previous afternoon he answered warily. Yes, the wolves had been disturbed but he knew of no reason, they had been fed and would normally have settled quietly. Were there many people about at the time, Holmes asked him. No he said, it was getting on for closing time and the season for visitors had not yet begun. Holmes asked if he might see the cage.

The man nodded and led us to an empty cage where the bars and wire netting had been temporarily boarded up. Holmes looked around the public area. He asked him again if there was anyone about at the time. The man shrugged. There was someone, he conceded reluctantly. A man had stood looking at the wolves for some time. A crackpot who had talked to them in some strange dialect but had turned away when the Keeper had taken a look at him. Holmes asked the man to describe him. A tall, gaunt man, the Keeper told him, pale, very pale, with sickly red rimmed eyes.

The man cheered up when he told us of Berserker's reappearance. Apparently the animal had been sleeping outside the cage when the Keeper arrived for duty that morning. It had been in some sort of scrape, he said, for there were cuts on its head and shards of broken glass in its fur. The Superintendent was quite ruffled that he had not been informed of this. We were shown the animal. It lay in the sun licking a paw, indifferent to the onlookers.

We returned to the house with heavy hearts. The curtains were closed and a wreath draped with black crepe hung on the door. Mina, dressed in black, and looking pale and tired, had some news for us.

The terrible events of the night before had restored her husband's memory. It is, of course, not uncommon for a shock to have this effect on an amnesiac. He was anxious to see us and Holmes was clearly keen to see him.

I was agreeably surprised to find him dressed and sitting in a chair when we entered the bedroom.

Though looking far from well it was obviously a progressive step to be out from the womb-like security of the bed.

There was, of course, a fearfulness about his speech when he spoke of Count Dracula's 'presence' but he became gradually more assured when he realised that we believed him and were not merely humouring him.

Mina and he held hands as he recalled some of the horrors of his time at Castle Dracula. I agreed with Holmes that he should be encouraged to talk these things out. My poor niece trembled visibly at his story. At length, Holmes touched on the purpose of his journey. Strangely these matters had faded from his memory, overwhelmed, no doubt, by the vivid experiences that led from them, but he slowly began to piece together the details. He had been commissioned by letter from Count Dracula to acquire a property for him, it had had to be an old property of dignity commensurate with the nobility of the Count's family. Janos had recognised that Constanza House, for that was the name of the neighbouring property, was such a place. He recalled, in halting fashion, the Count's words of satisfaction at his description of it:

"I am glad that it is old and large. I rejoice that there is a chapel of old times. We Transylvanian nobles love not to think that our bones may be amongst the common dead. I seek not gaiety or mirth, not the bright voluptuousness of sunshine and sparkling waters. I love the shade and the shadows and would be alone with my thoughts when I may." The talking began to weary the young man and I was relieved when Holmes suggested that he should rest.

That night after supper we received a visitor, or perhaps I should say Holmes received a visitor. In his correspondence with Brother Arminius he had been put in touch with a solemn young monk from an ancient monastery on the outskirt of the city. Brother Tamas was a tall, gaunt figure, his pale face shadowed by the heavy cowl that covered his head.

The low gas-lights accentuated the severity of his awesome garb. The servants genuflected as he passed with Holmes and I to the room which the undertaker had transformed into a small chapelle ardente. There was a wilderness of beautiful white flowers and death was made as little repulsive as might be. The end of the winding sheet was laid over Lucy's face. When Holmes bent over and turned it gently back, I was started at the beauty before us. The tall wax candles showed sufficient light to note it well. All her loveliness had come back to her in death, and the hours that had passed, instead of leaving traces of 'decay's effacing fingers' had but restored the beauty of life, till it was hard to believe that one was looking at a corpse.

Holmes and I stood back as Brother Tamas said a prayer for the dead. He then went into a whispered conversation with Holmes, who left the room for a few moments to return carrying a small parcel of fresh garlic flowers. I was astonished to see the young monk assist Holmes as they placed the flowers among the others on and around the bed. Then Holmes took a small golden crucifix from his pocket and handed it to the monk. I learned later that it was Lucy's personal crucifix which Holmes had found among her possessions. Brother Tamas blessed it and placed it over her mouth.

As Brother Tamas bade us good night I was touched to observe one of the maids pass silently along the passage to enter the room where Lucy lay. Devotion is so rare and here is a poor girl putting aside the terrors associated with death to watch alone by the bier of the mistress she loved.

Holmes stepped out into the night to see the monk into the carriage which had awaited him. When he returned we had a last smoke together before turning in. My friend commented on the holy man's belief that the crucifix would ward of the evil spirits. He observed, with grim humour, that in the 'Magia Posthuma' and the 'Phlegon de Mirabilibus' there were many recorded instances of the ancient practise of driving a stake through the heart and removing the head.

When I protested that as a Christian I could never condone such a belief he remarked calmly:

"I once heard an interesting definition of faith – 'that which enables us to believe things which we know to be untrue!'"

With that he tapped out his pipe and bade me sleep well.

I certainly slept, for the last few days and nights had been wearying. I was barely awake when Holmes came into my room.

"I fear our monastic friend's ministrations were not put to the test," he declared.

I rubbed the sleep out of my eyes and sat up.

"What on earth do you mean?" I asked.

He opened his hand to reveal the gold crucifix.

"This was stolen in the night."

"How stolen," I asked, "since you have it now?"

"Because I got it back from the wretch who stole it, one of the serving girls. Her punishment will surely come, though not through me."

As he withdrew from the room he said ominously:

"It is too late – or too early."

When Sandor came that evening to pay his last respects it was our sad duty to attend upon him. The two coffins, that of father and daughter, were side by side. The young man stood before Dr Westenra's coffin and gave a respectful salute. He crossed to Lucy's coffin and I lifted the lawn from her face. Oh, how beautiful she was. Every hour seemed to be enhancing her beauty. Sandor fell to his knees, trembling as with an ague.

"Is she really dead?" he asked in a whisper.

I assured him that sadly she was. With that he stood and looked at her again lovingly and long before taking her dead hand in his and kissing it and bending over to kiss her forehead. With that we withdrew and shortly afterwards I went to the kitchen where the undertaker's men were waiting. I told them to proceed with the preparations and screw down the coffins.

We dined together and all three spent the night there with Mina and Janos.

I slept a little myself but I know that Holmes did not retire until dawn. He went to and fro, as if patrolling the house, and was never out of sight of the room where Lucy and her father lay. The odour of the garlic flowers, strewn amongst lily and rose, gave off a heavy, overpowering smell into the night.

Next day our small cortege was joined by Dr Lukacs and members of the staff at the asylum, together with dignitaries from the city's medical fraternity, friends of the family and many of Lucy's friends from student days who might well have been guests at her wedding. Janos attended with Mina at his side. He cut a sad figure, his mourning clothes accentuating his paleness and the premature greying of his hair.

Afterwards Dr Lukacs told us of another disturbance at the asylum on the previous afternoon. Renfield had been returned to his room from the padded cell though under close supervision. He had become agitated and had sat crouched in the confines of his window shouting and screaming at some activity he sensed to be happening at Constanza House.

Renfield's shouts had been much of the order of previous occasions, begging "The Master" to save him, begging "The Master" not to desert him.

Out of curiosity Dr Lukacs had asked the Gateman on duty if he had seen any activity on the neighbouring estate and the man had replied that a carter's wagon had been driven up to the house and on its return had been laden with some wooden boxes.

I felt a sense of relief as I listened to the doctor's account. Perhaps, I thought, this time we have driven him away. But Holmes was not so easily assured.

In the days that followed I felt it behoved me to attend upon my niece and her husband. Janos, like many an invalid, made slow progress toward recovery, but progress there certainly was. Mina told me that his nightmares were less and less, though sometimes she awoke to find him in a cold sweat, a look of terror in his eyes.

Holmes occupied himself with visits to the city, assuming the role of someone on The Grand Tour. It was only when he returned one evening, dangling a set of keys that I realised that his tourism had taken him into the city's underworld and that, in some thieves' kitchen, he had acquired the tools of the burglar's trade.

CHAPTER TWELVE

Next morning at breakfast Holmes proposed that we make a search of Constanza House. When I hesitated at the wisdom of such a venture in broad daylight, Holmes said that he meant that we would go under cover of darkness. I was about to say that that prospect was not altogether pleasing either when something in the daily newspaper distracted him:

"Hulloa, Watson," he declared, "exactly as I feared – but so soon, so soon!"

I recognised the red-hot energy which underlay Holmes's phlegmatic exterior when I saw the change that came over him. In an instant he was tense and alert, his eyes shining, his face set, his limbs quivering with eager activity.

"Listen to this, my friend," he said, his voice full of foreboding:

"Parents in the Krisztina district of the city have been increasingly alarmed by instances of young children straying from home or neglecting to return from play. The children have been too young to give any properly intelligible account of themselves, but the consensus of their excuses is that they have been with 'the beautiful lady.' It has always been late in the evening when they have been missed, and on two occasions the children have not been found until early in the following morning. It is generally supposed in the neighbourhood that, as the first child missed gave as his reason for being away that a 'beautiful lady' had asked him to come for a walk, the others had picked up the phrase and used it as the occasion served. This is the more natural as the favourite game of the little ones at present is luring each other away by wiles. There is, however, possibly a serious side to the question, for some of the children, indeed all who have been missed overnight, have been slightly torn or wounded in the throat. The wounds seem such as might be made by a rat or a small dog. The police of the division have been instructed to keep a sharp lookout for straying children, especially when very young, in and around the Krisztina district and for any stray dog which may be about!"

Holmes looked up at me with a twitch of smile on his drawn countenance:

"If you have quite finished breakfasting, I suggest we go into the city."

I had indeed quite finished, for I had lost all appetite for food.

We were in a cab on our way to the newspaper offices when Holmes bade the driver to stop. He hailed a paper-seller and obtained a copy of a late edition. Our cabby waited patiently for further orders while Holmes ran his eye over the front page before calling for us to be driven to the St Stephan Hospital. He then sat back and read me the news item he had found:

"'Beautiful Lady' Mystery. Another Child Injured. We have just received intelligence that another child, missed last night, was discovered early this morning wandering near Krisztina Korut. The child had the same tiny wound in the throat as has been noticed in other cases. He was taken to the St Stephan Hospital, where he is reported to be in a weak and emaciated condition. When partially restored he was able to tell the common story of being lured away by 'The Beautiful Lady.'"

We were received with surprisingly little delay when we sent in our cards to Dr Vajda, the Medical Superintendent. Holmes by his cynical glance once more acknowledged the advantages of my journals since they have been read so far afield.

The child was awake when we entered the ward. It had had a sleep and taken some food and altogether was going on well. Dr Vajda had the houseman remove the bandage from the throat and show us the punctures. There was no mistaking the similarity to those which had been on Lucy's throat. They were smaller and the edges looked fresher; that was all.

Dr Vajda said that he did not entirely agree with the theory that the wound may have been caused by a rat or small dog but was more inclined to believe that it had been caused by a bat, since they were quite numerous in that part of the city.

"Out of so many harmless ones," he said, "there may be some wild specimen from the South of a more malignant species. Some sailor may have brought one home and it managed to escape; or even from the Zoological Gardens a young one may have got loose, or one be bred from a vampire. These things do occur, you know. Only a few days ago a wolf got out."

Holmes told him blithely that yes, we had heard of that occasion.

Vajda nodded. As we moved away from the child's bedside, he said with a smile:

"Do you know the little mite asked nurse if he could go away – he wanted to play with 'The Beautiful Lady'!"

"I hope," said Holmes, "that when you are sending him home you will caution the parents to keep a strict watch over him. These fancies to stray are the most dangerous."

"Oh, I most certainly agree," said Dr Vajda. "But we intend to keep him here for a week at least; longer if the wound is not healed."

The doctor was most intrigued by my friend's interest in the matter. I told him that Holmes and I had been involved in something similar some years ago in Sussex and that it had been solved by Holmes to everyone's satisfaction. "Ah, yes," said Dr Vajda. "'The Sussex Vampire' in your marvellous Casebook! I must look at it when I get home. My wife will be very interested."

I could see that Holmes wanted to be on his way before social invitations were proffered so I muttered something about the mounting cost of our hired cab and we slipped away.

That evening after Holmes had made several somewhat sinister purchases in the market place we dined in the garden of an old tavern in Krisztina. The simple tables were bedecked under the large plane trees, a Hungarian version of the Viennese Grinzing district. The melancholy music of a small wandering Gypsy orchestra did little to lift our spirits.

Holmes insisted that we should eat since we had a long night ahead of us. I had little appetite but did dispose of a warming goulash, a couple of home-grown peaches and a fair sampling of a strong country wine.

Although Holmes was as fond as I of first-class restaurants like the Cafe Royal, Simpson's in the Strand; Marcini's or The Criterion, for him the intake of food was more a matter of sensible discipline. He chose carefully and ate well but one got the impression that it was more a duty than a pleasure.

And, of course, he had that marvellous gift of detachment. Whilst I was filled with gloom at the prospect ahead of us he was able to discourse cheerfully about the history of the district and its famed zoldvendeglo or 'greenery restaurants.'

When we left, the place was full of the local habitués whose late-night gaiety had even enthused the musicians to play spirited waltzes and polkas.

As we approached the cemetery the scattered street lamps made the darkness greater when we were outside their individual radius. At last we reached the wall of the cemetery and climbed over.

With some difficulty – for it was very dark – we found the Westenra tomb. Holmes produced his skeleton keys, an irony that was not lost upon us, and began to work on the lock. It was relatively simple and in moments he swung back the creaky door. He stood aside for me, an unwelcome courtliness on such a ghastly occasion. He followed me quickly and drew the door to, after carefully ascertaining that the lock was a falling, and not a spring one. In the latter case we should be in a bad plight. Then he fumbled in his bag of purchases and taking out a match-box and a piece of candle, proceeded to make a light.

The tomb in the daytime, and when wreathed with fresh flowers, had looked gruesome enough; but now, some days afterwards, when the flowers hung lank and dead; their whites turned to rust and their greens to browns; when the spider and the beetle had resumed their accustomed dominance; when time-discoloured stone, and dust-encrusted mortar, and rusty, dank iron, and tarnished brass, and clouded silver plating gave back the feeble glimmer of a candle, the effect was more miserable and sordid than could have been imagined. It conveyed irresistibly the idea that life – animal life – was not the only thing which could pass away.

Holmes went about his work systematically. Holding his candle so that he could read the coffin plates, and so holding it that the sperm dropped in white patches which congealed as they touched the metal, he made assurance of Lucy's coffin. Another search in his bag and he took out a turnscrew.

Straightaway he began taking out the screws, and finally lifted off the lid, showing the casing of lead beneath. The sight was almost too much for me, though as a medical man I am hardly unfamiliar with death. It seemed to be as much an affront to the dead as it would have been to have stripped off her clothing in her sleep whilst living. I actually stayed Holmes's hand for a moment.

He only said: "You shall see," and again, fumbling in his bag, took out a tiny fret-saw. Striking the turnscrew through the lead with a swift downward stab, which made me wince, he made a small hole, which was, however, big enough to admit the point of the saw. I had expected a rush of gas from the week-old corpse. We doctors, who have had to study our dangers, have to become accustomed to such things, and I drew back toward the door. But Holmes did not stop for a moment; he sawed down a couple of feet along the lead coffin, and then across; and down the other side. Taking the edge of the loose flange, he bent it back toward the foot of the coffin, and holding up the candle into the aperture, motioned me to look.

I drew near and looked. The coffin was empty.

Though I had feared such a thing it was a considerable shock.

"Well?" said Holmes.

I shook my head. Gruesome though such a thought would be, I would have rather believed her body had been snatched for some awful purpose but I knew in my heart it was not so.

Holmes replaced the lid and turned the screws once more. Methodical as ever, he replaced his tools in the bag and blew out the candle, replacing it too in the bag. By then I had the door open and we went out. Holmes locked the tomb. Then we took up positions on opposite sides of the cemetery. I took my place behind a yew-tree and I watched his dark figure moving away until the intervening headstones and trees hid him from my sight.

It was a lonely vigil. Just after I had taken my place I heard a distant clock strike twelve, and in time came one and two. I was chilled and unnerved. I was too cold and too sleepy to be keenly observant, and not sleepy enough to betray my trust; so altogether I had a dreary, miserable time.

Suddenly, as I turned, I thought I saw something like a white streak, moving between two dark yew-trees at the side of the cemetery farthest from the tomb; at the same time a dark mass moved from Holmes's side of the ground and hurriedly went toward it. Then I too moved; but I had to go around headstones and railed-off tombs, and I stumbled over graves. The sky was overcast, and somewhere far off an early cock crew. A little way off, beyond the line of scattered juniper-trees, which marked the pathway to the church, a white dim figure flitted in the direction of the tomb. The tomb itself was hidden by trees, and I could not see where the figure disappeared. I heard the rustle of actual movement where I had first seen the white figure, and coming over, found Holmes holding in his arms a small child.

"Is it wounded?" I asked fearfully.

"We shall see," he replied moving swiftly towards the wall of the cemetery. When we were on the other side and a little distance away we went into a clump of trees and struck a match.

The child was without mark or a scratch of any kind. "We were just in time," said Holmes thankfully.

Carrying the child further toward a more inhabited part of the district, we decided that we could not take it to a police station or we would have to give account of our movements during the night.

We decided to place it where an early riser or better still a police patrol might find the sleepy little lad. Meanwhile we would wait, hidden, to be sure of its safe recovery. At length we heard the heavy tramp of a policeman and watched and waited until he saw it as he flashed his lantern to and fro. We heard his exclamation of astonishment and moved away silently. We got a cab in the restaurant district though I hardly think we were taken for late-night revellers.

CHAPTER THIRTEEN

We rested for a few hours though sleep, when it came, was fitful and disturbed. Mina and Janos waited expectantly for news from us but we had already decided that they should be spared as much pain as possible. As we were putting on our coats to depart once more around midday Mina took me aside to ask me if we had seen the reports about the straying children and 'The Beautiful Lady'. I said that we had and that Holmes and I were investigating the matter.

I noticed that Janos stood back a little but I feared that he was well aware of everything that was going on.

It was afternoon when we returned to the cemetery. There was a funeral in progress and Holmes ascertained that it was the last of four that day.

We assumed the role of relatives tending a grave, meanwhile watching the dispersal of the sad retinue. At length the cemetery was closed for the day and we were able to make progress despite the perils of the law which we were incurring in our unhallowed work. At times I tried to pretend that there was a desperate absurdity about it all. Outrageous as it was to open a leaded coffin, to see if a woman dead a week ago was really dead, surely it was folly to open the tomb again when we had seen, with our own eyes, that the coffin was empty. But, of course, I knew that there was no alternative.

Holmes opened the vault and again courteously motioned for me to precede. The place was not so gruesome as the previous night but, oh, how unutterably mean-looking when the sunshine streamed in. Holmes walked over to Lucy's coffin, and I followed. He bent over and again forced back the leaden flange; and then a shock of dismay shot through me.

There lay Lucy, seemingly just as we had seen her the night before her funeral. She was, if possible, more radiantly beautiful than ever; and I could not believe that she was dead. The lips were red, nay redder than before; and on the cheeks was a delicate bloom.

Holmes and I exchanged looks before he put over his hand, and in a way which made me shudder, pulled back the dead lips and showed the white teeth.

"See," he said, "see, they are even sharper than before. With this and this" – and he touched one of the canine teeth and that below it – "the little children can be bitten."

Holmes quietly replaced the lid and stepped away from the coffin.

He spoke in a quiet, matter-of-fact way:

"Here we are faced with something different from all record. Here is some dual life. She was bitten by the Vampire when she was in a trance, poor child, walking in her sleep. In that way he could best come to take more blood. In a trance she died and in a trance she is Un-Dead. So it is that she differs from all human kind. It is the common belief that when the Un-Dead sleep at 'home'," and here he made a sweep of his arm to designate what to a vampire was 'home', "their faces show what they are, but this sweet girl that was, would go back to the nothingness of the common dead. There is no malignity there. It would be a kindness to kill her in her sleep."

"How would you do this bloody work?" I asked.

"Her head should be cut off, her mouth filled with garlic and a stake be driven through her heart."

It made me shudder to think of so mutilating her body. And yet the feeling was not so strong as I had expected. I was, in fact, beginning to shudder at the presence of this being, this Un-Dead, as Holmes called it, and to loathe it. I felt that I had to leave that terrible place, to get some clean, fresh air, out of that dank place of rotting flowers and crawling insects.

Holmes followed me out into the waning sun-light, carefully locking the door of the vault.

We stood there surrounded by death; the silent monuments looking down upon us, the grim reaper and the angels of death.

"Perhaps this would be best," he said, as if thinking aloud. "If I did now, this moment, what I think to be best, I would do the terrible thing I described to you, but there are other things which will surely follow and we will need help if we are to destroy the awful instigator of this tragedy. She has not yet taken a life, but that is a matter of time. Sandor was her betrothed and when I asked swore to join forces with us, whatever the costs, for Lucy's sake. We must tell him what we know and perhaps Mina and Janos, too. I know that she is aware of the reports of the straying children."

I was hardly surprised as I knew well enough that little escaped his attention.

There was something about young Sandor's demeanour when he arrived that evening at the Westenra house that had prepared him, in some way, for the terrible facts that we were to lay before him. Janos had insisted on being present as if he, too, had some grim foreboding. Mina sat by his side, pale and trembling.

When Holmes finished speaking there was a long silence before Sandor got to his feet and spoke quietly and evenly. His faith he told us could not allow him to condone such a desecration of his love.

Holmes nodded solemnly.

"That I understand," he said, "but surely your faith could not condone the death of a single child, let alone the deaths of countless children."

"No, Mr Holmes," he replied, "it would not, but tell me, please tell me, what am I to do?"

Holmes then related something of his conversation with Brother Arminius when we took Janos to the monastery. He cited the learned deliberations of clerics long dead and of contemporary thinking on this ghastly phenomena. Finally he asked the young soldier if he would take counsel from Brother Tamas. Sandor agreed but with a deep sigh of anguish for which I pitied him.

Brother Tamas was at benediction when we arrived. We sat quietly in the rear pews as the service ended and the brothers filed out down the aisle singing their haunting chant. The novices began their task of extinguishing the altar candles, steadily increasing the gloom of the ancient chapel.

Brother Tamas returned and whispered something to Holmes who, in turn, told us to wait. He went with Brother Tamas, and we waited in silence, with Sandor kneeling at prayer. At length we heard the tread of their steps. Brother Tamas, tall and gaunt, was cloaked and cowled and had in his hands a bag made of purple velvet which bore the gold imprint of the crucifix. Holmes beckoned us to follow and we made our way to a carriage summoned by the Abbot.

It was just before midnight when we climbed over the low wall into the cemetery. The monk had not spoken during the journey but had fingered his rosary in silent prayer. The driver was told to wait in the square, shuttered and silent, that we had passed through a short time back.

Once more we entered the vault and went through the ritual of removing the coffin lid. Sandor was aghast when he saw the rent in the lead covering, the blood rushed to his face but as quickly fell away again. The monk stood silently, displaying no evident emotion. Holmes forced back the leaden flange and we looked in – the coffin was empty. Sandor recoiled in horror. Brother Tamas crossed himself and put an arm around the young man as he staggered out of the vault.

Holmes wasted no time in replacing the flange and screwing down the coffin lid. I waited in the doorway. The air seemed fresh and pure after the terror of the vault. How sweet it was to see the clouds race by, and the brief gleams of the moonlight between the scudding clouds crossing and passing like the gladness and sorrow of a man's life; how sweet it was to breathe the fresh air, that had no taint of death and decay.

When Holmes finished relocking the door, the silent monk loosened the strings on his purple bag and proceeded to rub a kind of paste on the surrounds of the door. Holmes told me quietly that it was made up of fragments of The Host, for which the Abbot had granted a special Indulgence. It was an answer that appalled what little scepticism remained in me and Holmes refrained from any comment.

Holmes assigned us our places for the long watch and we settled quietly. Brother Tamas spent some time talking, with Sandor, so that he, too, became resolved to the task before us. Apprenticed though I was to this watching horror I felt my heart sink within me. I pitied poor Sandor. Never did tombs look so ghastly white; never did cypress or yew or juniper so seem the embodiment of funereal gloom; never did tree or grass wave or rustle so ominously; never did bough creak so mysteriously; and never did the far-away howling of dogs send such a woeful presage through the night.

Time passed with aching slowness until I heard a hiss from my colleague and saw him move slightly forward. Far down the avenue of yews we saw a white figure advance – a dim white figure which held something dark at its breast. The figure stopped, and at that moment a ray of moonlight fell between the masses of driving clouds and showed in startling prominence a woman, dressed in the cerements of the grave. We could not see the face, for it was bent down over what we saw to be a fair-haired child. There was a pause and a sharp little cry, such as a child gives in sleep, or a dog as it lies before the fire and dreams. We were starting forward, but Holmes's warning hand, seen by us as he stood behind a yew-tree, kept us back; and then as we looked the white figure moved forward again. It was now near enough for us to see clearly, and the moonlight still held. My own heart grew cold as ice, and I could hear the gasp of Sandor as we recognised the features of Lucy Westenra.

Lucy Westenra, but yet how changed. The sweetness was changed to adamantine, heartless cruelty, and the purity to voluptuous wantonness.

Holmes stepped out, and, obedient to his gesture, we stood in line ranged before the door of the tomb. Holmes lit his torch and by the concentrated beam that fell on Lucy's face we could see that the lips were crimson with fresh blood and that the stream had trickled over her chin and had stained the purity of her lawn death-robe.

We shuddered with horror. I could see by the light that even Holmes recoiled at the creature before us.

When Lucy – I call the thing that stood facing us Lucy because it bore her shape – saw us she drew back with an angry snarl, such as a cat gives when taken unawares; then her eyes ranged over us. Lucy's eyes in form and colour; but Lucy's eyes unclean and full of hell-fire, instead of the pure, gentle orbs we knew. At that moment the remnant of my affection passed into hate and loathing; had she then to be killed, I could have done it as if I were on the field of battle. As she looked, her eyes blazed with unholy light and the face became wreathed with a voluptuous smile. Oh, God, how it made me shudder to see it!

With a careless motion, she flung to the ground, callous as a devil, the child that up to now she had clutched strenuously to her breast, growling over it as a dog growls over a bone. The child gave a sharp cry and lay there moaning. There was a cold bloodedness in the act which wrung a groan from Sandor; when she advanced to him with outstretched arms and a wanton smile, he fell back and hid his face in his hands.

She still advanced however, and with a languorous, voluptuous grace.

"Come to me, Sandor," she said. "Leave these others and come to me. My arms are hungry for you. Come, and we can rest together. Come, my husband, come!"

There was something diabolically sweet in her tones – something of the tingling of glass when struck. Sandor seemed to come under her spell; moving his hands from his face, he opened wide his arms. She was moving toward them when Brother Tamas stepped forward and held between them his simple crucifix. She recoiled from it and, with a suddenly distorted face full of rage dashed past us as if to enter the tomb.

When within a foot or two of the door she stopped as if arrested by some irresistible force. Then she turned and her face was shown in the harsh beam of Holmes's torch, held as steady as a rock. Never did I see such baffled malice on a face; and never, I trust, shall such ever be seen again by mortal eyes. The beautiful colour became livid, the eyes seemed to throw out sparks of hell-fire, the brows were wrinkled as though the folds of the flesh were the coils of Medusa's snakes, and the lovely, bloodstained mouth grew to an open square, as in the passion masks of the Greeks and Japanese. If ever a face meant death we saw it at that moment.

And so for full half a minute, which seemed an eternity, she remained between the lifted crucifix and the sacred closing of her means of entry. Holmes broke the silence, addressing Sandor:

"Well, my young friend, are we to proceed?" he asked quietly, a resolute steadiness in his voice.

"Do as you will, do as you will," Sandor replied. "There can be no horror like this ever any more!"

Brother Tamas looked at Holmes who nodded solemnly in return. The monk stepped forward to the door of the tomb and with a silken cloth from his bag he began to wipe the surrounds. As he did so we became aware of a mist rising stealthily around us and the surrounding tombs. In a few moments we were all unseen by one another. In less than a minute the mist sank away and we heard the child's plaintive cry. Of Lucy there was no sign.

I examined the child by the light of Holmes's torch. Mercifully the harm was not as great as might have been. Sandor ran ahead for the coachman and we sped through the streets to the hospital of St Stephan. Holmes, Sandor and I waited while the monk handed the child to one of the nursing nuns. Whatever words were exchanged between them, the nun did as she was bid. In the sickly light of the entrance hall I saw her respond to the monk's blessing before she hurried away down the hall with her precious charge.

It was daylight when we arrived at the entrance to the cemetery. The cemetery-keeper was at breakfast at his cottage by the gate. Again a few words from Brother Tamas sufficed and the man, embarrassed by his lack of uniform, hastened to unlock the gates. We went on foot down the tree-lined avenue after first waiting for the keeper to close the gates once more. Holmes carried a long leather bag, somewhat like a cricketing bag, which he had taken with him to the monastery and had left meanwhile with our driver.

When we reached the tomb it was dappled in morning sunlight and seemed innocent of what had taken place before dawn.

Holmes unlocked the tomb and we went in, closing the door behind us. Then Holmes took from his bag a lantern which he lit and also two wax candles which, when lighted, he stuck, by melting their own ends, on other coffins, so that they might give sufficient light to work by.

When the coffin was opened and the leaded flange drawn back the body lay there in all its death-beauty. I felt nothing but loathing for the foul Thing which had taken Lucy's shape without her soul. Presently Sandor spoke:

"Is this really Lucy's body, or a demon in her shape?"

Holmes waited for Brother Tamas to speak:

"It is her body, my son, and yet not it. Soon you will see her as she was and is." He nodded solemnly to Holmes who silently began his preparations.

The Thing seemed like a nightmare of Lucy as she lay there; the pointed teeth, the bloodstained, voluptuous mouth, the whole carnal and unspiritual appearance, seeming like a devilish mockery of Lucy's sweet purity.

Holmes in his methodical manner took the various contents from his bag and placed them ready for use. First he took out a soldering iron and some plumbing solder, and then a small oil-lamp, which gave out, when lit in a corner of the tomb, gas which burned at fierce heat with a blue flame; then a set of knives, which he placed to hand; and last a round wooden stake, some two and half or three inches thick and about three feet long. One end was hardened by charring in the fire and sharpened to a fine point. With this stake came a heavy hammer, such as in households is used in the coal-cellar for breaking the lumps.

Once more Holmes paused and looked at the solemn Brother Tamas, his white face shadowed by the heavy cowl around his head.

The monk spoke to Sandor but his words were for us all:

"It is out of the lore and experience of the ancients and all of those who have studied the powers of the Un-Dead, that when they become such, there comes with the change the curse of immortality; they cannot die but must go on age after age adding new victims and multiplying the evils of the world; for all that die from the preying of the Un-Dead become themselves Un-Dead, and prey on their kind. And so the circle goes on ever widening, like the ripples from a stone thrown in the water."

"My son if you had met that embrace last night you would in time, when you died, have become Nosferatu and would for all time have made more of those Un-Deads that fill us with horror. The career of this unhappy child, Lucy, has but just begun. Those children whose blood she has sucked are as yet not much the worse but if she lives on, Un-Dead, more and more they will lose their blood. By her power over them, they will come to her and so she will draw their blood. But if she dies in truth they will live on and in time die naturally. Most blessed of all, when this now Un-Dead be made to rest as truly dead, then her soul will at last be free.

Instead of working the wickedness of the night and growing more debased by day in the assimilation of it, she shall take her place among the Angels. It will be a blessed hand that strikes the blow that sets her free."

Without a word Sandor stepped forward and took the stake and the hammer from Holmes.

"Brave man," my friend said with quiet assurance, "A moment's courage and it is done."

"Tell me what I am to do," the young man asked.

"Take the stake in your left hand, ready to place the point over the heart, and the hammer in your right and be ready when Brother Tamas bids you to strike."

Brother Tamas opened his worn, black prayer-book:

"I shall read The Prayer for the Dead and when I raise my hand you will strike in God's name so that all shall be well with the dead that we love, and that the Un-Dead shall pass away."

Sandor made ready and the monk intoned the solemn prayer. When the moment came Sandor struck with all his might. The Thing in the coffin writhed; and a hideous, blood-curdling screech came from the opened red lips. The body shook and quivered and twisted in wild contortions; the sharp white teeth champed together till the lips were cut and the mouth was smeared with crimson foam. But Sandor did not falter. He looked like a figure of Thor as his untrembling arm rose and fell driving deeper and deeper the mercy-bearing stake, whilst the blood from the pierced heart welled and spurted up around it. His face was set, and high duty seemed to shine through it. And then the writhing and the quivering of the body became less and the teeth ceased to champ and the face to quiver. Finally it lay still.

Sandor's task was over. The hammer fell from his hand. He reeled and would have fallen had not Holmes caught him. Great drops of sweat sprang out of his forehead and his breath came in broken gasps. For a few moments we were so taken with him that we did not look toward the coffin. It was Brother's Tamas's administration of the blessing that directed our eyes once more to the corpse.

There in the coffin lay no longer the foul Thing that had so appalled us, but Lucy as we had seen her in life, with her face of unequalled purity and sweetness, with, as we had also seen in life, the traces of care and pain and waste. One and all we felt that the holy calm that lay like sunshine over the wasted face and form was only an earthly token and symbol of the peace that was to reign forever.

She is no longer the devil's Un-Dead," said the monk. "She is God's true dead whose soul is with Him."

Brother Tamas led Sandor out into the day-light to wait upon us while we removed the head and filled the mouth with garlic. Holmes soldered up the leaded coffin and I helped him screw on the coffin-lid. We gathered up the implements and went out to find the air sweet, the sun shining and the birds singing, as if all nature were tuned to a different pitch.

"One step of our work is done," said Holmes. "One of the most harrowing to us all. But we must seek

out the author of all this sorrow and stamp him out.
I have clues that we can follow but it may be a long
task and difficult and there is danger in it."

The warmth of the sun did nothing to help with the
chill I felt within me at Holmes's timely reminder.

CHAPTER FOURTEEN

I think Holmes was as weary as I when we returned to the Westenra house shortly before mid-day. Brother Tamas had returned to the monastery and Sandor to his quarters. Janos was in the study with a lawyer for the estate. Since he was a relative of the family, cousin to poor Lucy, he was endeavouring to assist in settling affairs. It was commendable and encouraging but one hoped he would not overtax himself.

When Holmes enquired after my niece, Janos said that Dr Lukacs had called for coffee and that afterwards Mina had gone with him to the asylum for a visit.

"What an extraordinary thing –" I began but Holmes interrupted me:

"Not, by any chance, to see that fellow Renfield?" Janos blinked a little before he stammered:

"I … I … it was mentioned."

Holmes gave a brief smile and turned to me:

"Perhaps we should look in on the wretched chap, mmm?" I sensed that it was hardly a question.

"Yes," I said, not wishing to disturb Janos "why not? It would seem the charitable thing to do."

We made our brief excuses to the family lawyer for our brief interruption and left the house. I noticed that Janos was at the study window as we made off across the lawn.

"This is all rather strange," Holmes murmured.

"Very," I replied "Janos is clearly worried."

"Mmm," Holmes said, "we must not appear to be in any way hurried."

Thus we were obliged to take our time.

We were already familiar to the staff and when we asked to present our compliments to Dr Lukacs we were informed that he was on the wards and an attendant was assigned to accompany us.

Once more we were on our way to the section in which Renfield was detained. When we turned the corridor and were a few yards distant, Holmes signalled to Dr Lukacs not to comment on our arrival. He answered with the merest acknowledgement. He and Mina were standing by the open aperture of the cell door and Renfield was evidently on the other side. Mina turned for a moment but she too accepted Holmes's signal without showing any sign.

"Who is there?" Renfield asked, an alertness in his voice.

"Bruno," said Dr Lukacs, "with medicine for Mr Kovac."

"Huh, none for me, eh?" Renfield replied.

"I don't believe you are due any at present," said Dr Lukacs easily.

"You were saying, Mr Renfield," said Mina gently.

There was a long silence before he spoke:

"You must leave that house, madam ..."

"But why?" asked Mina, a note of anxiety in her voice.

"Who is there?" Renfield asked sharply. "That is not Bruno."

Dr Lukacs smiled patiently and beckoned to the attendant who, like ourselves, was out of the lunatic's vision. Bruno stepped forward.

"Huh" said Renfield, seemingly mollified. Bruno turned and walked away evidently well versed in the behaviour of Renfield.

"Why must I leave?" Mina repeated.

There was another pause.

"You must leave that house, madam. It is for the best."

"Thank you for your concern," said Mina, "now, Mr Renfield, you were going to tell me of your beliefs."

"Mmm, you are very persuasive, madam, but I hardly think my 'beliefs' as you put it, will appeal. You see I was a man who had such strange ideas that perhaps it was no wonder that my friends were alarmed, and insisted on my being put under control. I fancied that life was a positive and perpetual entity, and that by consuming a multitude of live things, no matter how low in the scale of creation, one might and indefinitely prolong life. At times I held the belief so strongly that I actually tried to take human life."

Mina was silent, appalled no doubt by the horror of this strange philosophy spoken with such awesome saneness.

"I see you are shocked, madam, and well you might be. Leave that place, madam."

Mina recovered herself and spoke, though querulously:

"Goodbye, Mr Renfield, I hope we meet again under happier circumstances."

"Goodbye, my dear," he said, with an odd gentleness in his voice. "I pray God I may never see your sweet face again. May He bless you and keep you."

With that he must have turned away. Dr Lukacs tapped Mina on the shoulder and led her away. We, in turn, followed as silently as possible.

None of us spoke until we were well out of earshot.

"What a sad, miserable creature," said Mina, "one would think he was harmless if one did not know otherwise."

"That is why he is under lock and key," said Dr Lukacs.

"Any more outbreaks of violence?" Holmes asked.

"No," the doctor replied, "he is back to his revolting habit of gorging on flies and spiders ..."

That evening Holmes called for a 'Council of War,' attended by Sandor, Mina, Janos and myself. We gathered in the library. Mina tried to conceal her nervousness by occupying herself with some needlework. I attempted to divert myself by playing a game of patience. Holmes spent some time in the meticulous preparation of his favourite clay before he began.

"That there is such a phenomena as the vampire is, for us, no longer a matter of superstition or legend since we have the proof of our own unhappy experience."

He looked at each of us and we all gave the same sad response.

"No one," he went on, "could have been more sceptical than I. A few weeks ago which of us here would have acknowledged such a possibility in these scientific, modern times? But if we acknowledge such a reality perhaps we should take it that the belief in the vampire's limitations as well as its exorcism rest on the same base."

Holmes paused to take a puff or two on his pipe.

"These beliefs have been held down the centuries, in ancient Greece, in Rome, throughout Europe, particularly here in the East and in India and China.

It is said that the vampire cannot die by the passing of time and that it flourishes when it battens on the blood of the living. We ourselves have seen that it can grow younger, that its faculties are recharged when its sustenance has been plentiful. It does not eat as living things do. It casts no shadow. It does not reflect on any mirrored surface. It has the strength of many in its hands. It can see in the dark and it can transform itself into other creatures – the dog that leapt ashore when the barge ran aground, the vampire bat.

It can summon the mists, create havoc and yet it is no more free than our madman in his cell.

Curiously, this unnatural phenomena has to obey certain natural laws. It cannot enter anywhere without at first some form of human assistance, though afterwards it can come and go as it pleases, but its power ceases with the coming of the day.

Only at certain times can it have limited freedom. The works I have consulted, compiled centuries apart, all tend to suggest that if it is not at the place it is bound for, it can only change itself at noon or at sunrise or at sunset.

The time for its destruction is when it is powerless, when it rests.

We learned from Brother Arminius, when the monks gave us shelter after our escape, that the Draculas were not all evil and that the Count cannot rest in soil barren of their holy memories. That is why we have to trace those boxes, dangerous though the task may be, until we find the one in which he has chosen to lie."

He fell silent and took the opportunity to re-light his clay.

"Should we not make a start tonight at Constanza House?" I asked.

Holmes nodded. "Just before dawn, I think. He may lead us to his place of rest."

It was agreed that Sandor should accompany Holmes and I but that Janos should, of course, stay with Mina. Janos argued energetically that it was his duty to come with us and his spirit certainly showed that he was well recovered.

We had a few hours sleep and assembled in the hall a little after four o'clock. Janos watched from the bedroom window as we set out for Constanza

House. We were armed with torches and Sandor had managed to acquire a couple of revolvers which Holmes insisted were best in the hands of the young officer and myself. Quite how conventional weapons could protect us from such phenomena was not willingly discussed. Holmes's skeleton keys were not well suited to the ancient, long disused locks but eventually one succeeded thanks to my friend's almost surgical dexterity. After a little play back and forth the bolt yielded and shot back with a rusty clang. It took two of us to push the heavy door, its hinges creaking, until we were able to enter.

In manus tuas, Domine!" Sandor whispered as he crossed himself at the threshold. We closed the door behind us before we lit our torches. The beams of light fell in all sorts of odd forms as the rays crossed each other, or the capacity of our bodies threw great shadows. I could not for the life of me throw off the feeling that there was someone else amongst us. I think the feeling was common to us all, for I noticed that my companions looked over their shoulders at every sound and every new shadow, just as I felt myself doing.

The whole place was thick with dust. The floor was seemingly inches deep, except where there were recent footsteps, in which on holding down my torch I could see the marks of hobnails where the dust was caked. The walls were fluffy and heavy with dust and in the corners were masses of spiders' webs, whereon the dust had gathered till they looked like old tattered rags as the weight had torn them partly down. On a table in the hall was a great bunch of keys, with a time-yellowed label on each. They had been used several times, for on the table were several similar rents in the blanket of dust, like those exposed when Holmes picked up the keys.

Holmes made an indication with his torch:

"I fancy the entrance to the chapel must be in this direction."

We moved off, staying fairly close together. After a few wrong turnings, for the old house was quite a maze of corridors, we found ourselves opposite a low, arched oaken door, ribbed with iron bands.

Holmes found the tagged key and, with a little trouble, unlocked the door. We were prepared for some unpleasantness, for as we were opening the door a faint, malodorous air seemed to exhale through the gaps, but I am quite sure none of us expected such an odour as we encountered. At least the ruined chapel at Castle Dracula had been opened to the sky but here the place was smaller and enclosed and the long disuse would have made the air stagnant and foul. There was an earthy smell, as of some dry miasma, which came through the fouler air. But as to the odour itself, it was not alone that it was composed of all the ills of mortality and with the pungent, acrid smell of blood, but it seemed as though corruption had become itself corrupt. Faugh! It is sickening to think of it. Every breath exhaled by that monster seemed to have clung to the place and intensified its loathsomeness.

Ordinarily the stench would have been overwhelming but the terrible purpose of our endeavours forced us on. The boxes were placed haphazardly in various parts of the chapel.

"The first thing is to see how many boxes are left," said Holmes. "We must then examine every hole and corner and see if we cannot get some clue as to what has become of the others."

There were only twenty-nine remaining of the fifty that we knew to have been taken from the barge.

We counted and recounted, our torches flitting over the evil looking caskets. Once I got the most awful sensation of fear. Seeing Sandor suddenly turn and look out of the vaulted door into the dark passage beyond, I looked too and for an instant my heart stood still. Somewhere, looking out from the shadow, I seemed to the see the highlights of the Count's evil face, the ridge of the nose, the red eyes, the red lips, the awful pallor. It was only for a moment. Sandor spoke in a hushed voice, forcing a thin chuckle:

"I thought I saw a face, but it was only the shadows."

Holmes and I exchanged looks.

My friend moved boldly towards the vaulted door, his torch piercing the darkness to illuminate the solid walls of the passage. There could be no hiding place, even for the Count. I took it that perhaps fear had overworked one's imagination.

A few minutes later I saw Sandor step suddenly back from a corner which he had been examining. We both followed his movements with our eyes for undoubtedly some added tension was growing on us. We saw a mass of phosphorescence which twinkled like stars. We instinctively drew back. The whole place was becoming alive with rats.

For a moment or two we stood appalled then Sandor whipped out his revolver and began firing at the teeming horde. They seemed to swarm over the place all at once, till the torch beams shining on their moving dark bodies and glittering, baleful eyes, made the place look like a bank of earth set with fireflies. I, too, drew my revolver and began firing into the mass of vile creatures. The noise of the ricocheting bullets and the mayhem they caused rapidly turned the horde and they vanished as quickly as they had appeared.

As the noise of our firing died away we heard once more the desperate wail of the siren coming from the asylum. Holmes nodded to me as if an agreement with my unspoken thoughts and we made our way out of the chapel and out through the corridors to the entrance hall.

"One lesson we have learned," he said as he led us out of the house, "is that the brute beasts at the Count's command are yet themselves not amenable to his spiritual powers for they ran pell-mell when you fired on them and their dead lay well and truly dead!"

CHAPTER FIFTEEN

Sandor came with us to the asylum and we soon found ourselves on the inevitable way to Renfield's room. The whole institution rang with the crazed voices of the other inmates, moaning, keening, screaming, deeply disturbed by some awful portent. Renfield lay in a glittering pool of blood, Dr Lukacs kneeling beside him.

It was at once apparent that he had received some terrible injuries; there seemed none of that unity of purpose between the parts of the body which marks even lethargic sanity. As the face was exposed we could see that it was horribly bruised, as though it had been beaten against the floor – indeed it was from the face wounds that the pool of blood originated.

Dr Lukacs took us in with a glance, unsurprised at our appearance:

"His back is broken. Both his right arm and leg and the whole side of his face are paralysed."

He stood up and move toward us, speaking quietly:

"I cannot understand it. He could mark his face like that by beating his head on the floor. I once saw a young woman do something similar before anyone could lay hands on her but that could not explain his broken back. If he fell awkwardly from his bunk it is just possible but for the life of me I cannot conceive how the two things could have occurred."

Holmes moved quietly around the room examining the window beyond the bars. It was possible for the inmate to open it to a limited extent and this had been done.

Holmes peered closely at the walls and the few items of furniture. He pointed out signs of disturbance and the thin spray of blood stains spattered here and there. All of this he did without speaking until he came back to where we were standing:

"Dr Lukacs," he began quietly, "I fancy you are well aware that we are investigating some strange happenings?"

The doctor nodded:

"Poor Westenra, before his death, gave me some indication. I knew him to be deeply worried and he was not a man to sensationalise."

"Quite," said Holmes. "Unfortunately we are not yet in a position to enlighten you but I can assure you that it is a matter of great urgency that Watson and I speak with this wretched creature before his demise and I fear that moment is not far off?"

Dr Lukacs looked at me:

"It is imminent, but I doubt whether he will regain the power of speech."

I looked down at poor Renfield. He was breathing stertorously, his eyelids flickering. He begun to mutter and groan. Suddenly his eyes opened. He seemed to stare at us all for several moments before he began to speak:

"You," he said, "you the Englishmen." His voice was weak. "You I will speak with, not the others."

Holmes and I looked at Dr Lukacs and at Sandor standing by the door. Sandor nodded his understanding and withdrew into the corridor. Lukacs looked directly at me:

"I leave him in your care, doctor."

With that he too went out into the corridor closing the door to lessen the noise of the other inmates. For some time Renfield breathed in a desperate, panting manner; his eyes became fixed in a wild helpless stare. He moved convulsively and said "I'll be quiet, doctor. I have had a dream, a terrible dream and it has left me so weak I cannot move."

I feared that he was already lost to us in his madness but Holmes spoke gently:

"Tell us your dream, Mr Renfield."

He seemed to focus on us again:

"Ah, yes, it is you. How good it is of you to be here. Give me some water, my lips are dry; and I shall try to tell you. I dreamed –". He stopped as if he might be falling into a faint. Luckily I had my small flask with me and I mixed it with some water and moistened his lips. It seemed his brain had been working in the interval for he looked at us piercingly and said:

"I must not deceive myself for it was no dream. Quick, sir, a little bit more brandy for I am dying. A few minutes and I must go back to death – or worse!"

I did as he asked and he went on:

"I have something I must say before I die; or before my poor crushed brain dies anyhow. You were here, I know you were, when that young lady visited me.

For a time, after she left, I felt a deep despair. Then there came a sudden peace to me. My brain seemed to become cool again. I looked out of my window and saw a mist gather. Then He came to the window as I had seen Him often before; but He was solid then, not a ghost, and His eyes were fierce like a man's when angry. He was laughing with His red mouth; the sharp white teeth glinting in the moonlight ... I would not ask Him to come in at first, though I knew He wanted to – just as He had all along. Then He began promising me things – not in words but by doing them."

"How?" asked Holmes quietly. "What things did he do?"

"By making them happen," said Renfield in a wondrous manner, "just as He used to send in the flies when the sun was shining. Great big fat ones with steel and sapphire on their wings; and big moths, in the night, with skull and cross-bones on their backs!"

"The Acherontia atrapos of the Sphinges," murmured Holmes, "The 'Death's Head moth!'"

"Yes!" said Renfield, "The 'Death's Head.' Then He began to tempt me with rats. Hundreds, thousands, millions of them, and every one a life; and dogs to eat them and cats, too. All lives. All red blood with years of life in it! And not mere buzzing flies. I laughed at Him, for I wanted to see what He could do. He beckoned me closer to the window. I looked out as He raised his arms and seemed to call out without using any words. A dark mass spread over the grass coming on like the shape of a flame of fire; and then He moved the mist to the right and the left and I could see that there were thousands of rats with their eyes blazing red – like His, only smaller. He held up His hand and they all stopped; and I thought He seemed to be saying: 'All these lives will I give you, ay, and many more and greater, through countless ages, if you will fall down and worship me!' And then a red cloud, like the colour of blood seemed to close over my eyes; and before I knew what I was doing, I found myself opening the window to Him:

'Come in, Lord and Master!' The rats were all gone but He slid in, though the window was only open a few inches, just as the Moon herself has often come in through the tiniest crack and has stood before me in all her size and splendour."

He looked up at me and I moistened his lips again. He nodded thankfully and went on:

"The mist was here in this room with Him. He turned on me, sneering. I felt myself anger. He went on as though He owned the place and I was no one. He did not even smell the same as He went by me. I tried to hold Him. I felt, I felt as though that young lady was here again. I felt that she was not the same, like tea after the pot has been watered." Renfield stopped. I was about to rise but Holmes restrained me with a firm grip and a finger against his lips.

Renfield spoke again: "I don't care for pale people, I like them to have lots of blood in them, and hers had all seemed to run out. I think that is what angered me. I suddenly felt that He had been taking the life from her. I grabbed Him hard for I have heard that madmen have the strength of ten and as I knew I was mad I resolved to use my power."

He paused again and I moistened his lips. His voice was weakening.

"I held tight," he went on, "and I thought I was going to win, for I wanted to stop Him taking any more of her life, till I saw his eyes. They burned into me and my strength became like water. When I tried to cling to Him, He raised me up and flung me down. Not once but again and again. There was a red cloud before me and a noise like thunder until the mist seemed to steal away under the door and I lay here in my own blood."

His voiced almost faded away with those last words. I moved to offer him more brandy but his eyes closed. After a time they opened again, fluttering wildly. A look of abject fear spread across his face before he slipped away into whatever fate awaited him on the other side.

Holmes moved to the window, staring out at the day-break. Constanza House could just be seen beyond the trees, the first rays of a red sun glinting on the roof-top.

"I wanted to stop him taking any more of her life ..." Holmes repeated.

He turned to me. "Leave that house" he told her ...

That crazed brain had unspoken communication with Dracula. Unspoken communication between the living, yes! Thought transference! But unspoken communication between the living – and the Un-

Dead. This is the power that I fear most in this whole desperate affair."

With that he glanced down at the twisted body of the dead maniac and walked out of the room.

Dr Lukacs nodded when Holmes told him that Renfield had passed away. He shook our hands solemnly and asked no questions. As we left he began to give orders to his staff for the removal of the body. Sandor followed us as we made our way down the long corridors with the hellish noises and the clanging of tin mugs against the metal doors. When we were clear of the building Holmes turned to the young man:

"If that poor wretch was right – and I fear he may have been – Mina is at grave risk."

Sandor crossed himself as he strode along with us on our way back to the Westenra house.

Mina was standing at the bedroom window as we approached. Her face was pale in the morning sunlight, her eyes strangely vacant, unseeing.

Sandor remained below as Holmes and I hurried up the stairs. I tapped on the door. There was no response. I tapped again, louder this time. Again no response. Holmes opened the door. Mina stood at the window with her back to us. There was no sign of Janos.

"Mina," I said gently, "Mina."

She seemed to give an involuntary shiver before she turned slowly towards us.

She summoned a wan smile. "Uncle John, Mr Holmes ... Good morning."

She advanced towards us. We were relieved to see that her white throat showed no signs of the dreaded marks.

"Is Janos with you?" she asked.

"No," I said, "perhaps he is downstairs already."

"Have you not read this note?" Holmes asked, moving to the mantelpiece and holding up a piece of paper.

"No, I ..." Mina seemed unable to answer.

"With your permission?" said Holmes.

"Yes, yes of course," she said but there was still a strange sense of distance in her speech.

"Dearest, I think I have remembered something that may be important. I tried to wake you but you were in a deep sleep. I will be back very soon perhaps before you awake. Your loving Janos ..."

Mina was much more awake now and frowned with concern:

"But he should not have gone alone!"

"No," said my friend gently, "he is a brave young fellow and headstrong, too."

"Don't worry, my dear," I said in a wretched display of confidence. "It is broad daylight and he is much recovered."

We were having a rather dismal breakfast when Holmes, who had been sitting by the window quietly smoking his pipe, got up and left the room. After a few moments I followed him. He was hurrying across the lawn to meet the returning Janos. When I reached them the young man was apologising to Holmes:

"I am sorry if I broke ranks but I remembered something I had seen at the Castle. A document about another property. I barely had the chance to see it before the Count removed it from my sight."

"But you remembered! Well done, my lad!" said Holmes.

"I was not absolutely sure so I went to see for myself," he said. "It is the place, a town house in the Leopold District behind the Opera House. It is shuttered and the paint is peeling but I am sure it is the place."

Holmes turned to me.

"We must go there at once," he said.

"But we can hardly break-in in broad daylight in the centre of the city," I cautioned.

"The very best time!" insisted Holmes. "Dignified city folk such as ourselves with perhaps a smartly uniformed Hussar and, maybe a carriage bearing his family crest?" He turned to look at Sandor who had joined us.

"That can be arranged," said Sandor.

"Good!" said Holmes, "and you, young man," said Holmes looking at Janos, "will stay here with your dear wife and cause her no more alarums ..."

We turned toward the breakfast room. Oddly, Mina had remained within but watched intently nevertheless.

"You are right, of course," said Janos, "I will not break ranks again."

He hurried into the house and Mina turned away from the window ready to greet him.

I had already agreed with Holmes that it would not be wise to tell Janos of our fears for Mina. A fitter man would have found it hard enough to bear.

Sandor obtained a rather splendid brougham and we arrived in style outside the townhouse. Holmes's ruse worked. While Sandor and I chatted amiably on the steps inside the small courtyard we gave cover to Holmes as he worked on the lock.

Meanwhile a pair of policeman paused to pass the time with the coachman, turning after a few moments to salute Sandor, who responded with dignity. I noted with relief that they moved off before Holmes succeeded with the lock and we entered the building.

Once more we were assailed by the vile smell of decay mixed with the pungency of blood. It seemed to emanate from the cellar and sure enough we found nine boxes filled with earth – but no Count Dracula. Holmes searched the place thoroughly with his torch. He espied the slight tilting of one of the boxes as though the ground was uneven. He was quickly down on hands and knees:

"Hulloa, what have we here?" he murmured. Straightening up he signalled to us to help him move the box a little. "Ease him over a few inches, gentlemen." We did so.

"Ahah! Quite a little cache," he said, carefully unfolding some documents. "I say Watson, jot down these addresses if you will be so kind."

I got out a pen and paper and followed his careful dictation. There were the addresses of two other properties in the city. He then examined some tagged keys.

"Fairly antiquated," he remarked. "I fancy the locks will be easy enough."

We replaced everything exactly as we had found it, leaving the box slightly atilt, before searching the rest of the house right up to the attic. There was nothing of significance, just the usual abandoned relics of former occupation; broken toys, threadbare rugs, some saddlery, rotten with age, and a few gardening implements.

When we were out in the street, Holmes decided we should dispense with the carriage since the new addresses were in less salubrious parts of the city.

"Look here, young man," he told Sandor. "It might be wise if you apply for some leave. Protecting Mina is going to be a full-time job, let along seeking out our foe."

Sandor assured us that would not be a problem. He was due some leave and his bereavement made it all the more possible.

With that he went off in his family brougham and we hailed a cab.

The first of the two addresses turned out to be an old summer house by the river. It was not much more than a shack with a deck overlooking the river which passed at the foot of an unkempt strip of garden. I went down to the water's edge while Holmes sought entry at the door leading from the deck. After a few moments I saw that he had been successful and went in myself.

The place was simply furnished if somewhat dilapidated and had presumably been sold with contents. Some of it had been pushed aside to make space for the boxes, six in all. Though the shutters were sagging from their hinges and the blinds were somewhat ragged the place was dim and almost free of sunlight. Again there was no sign of the Count.

Holmes sniffed the air:

"This would seem to be a bolt-hole the wretch has yet to use."

"Mmm, and all the better for that," I mused.

Holmes was anxious to be off.

"Let us hurry," he said, "Time is passing and we may yet find him at rest!"

It was, indeed, late in the day when we reached the second address. Already the sun was descending behind the buildings. Alas, we were in the wrong place for the spot where the property should have been was part of a site cleared for re-building.

We re-checked the address I had noted down. There seemed to be no mistake.

"The Post Office," said Holmes. "We need a directory!"

Fortunately we were able to pick up another cab and in minutes we were pouring over a directory of Budapest.

There were two streets of the same name but in different districts. The cabbie waited for us and in minutes we reached the street we were after. We paid him off at the entrance to the street and reconnoitred on foot. It was dusk now. We found the house, detached and set back from the pavement by a small overgrown garden, with an agent's For Sale sign still in place. Again I kept look-out while Holmes went down a side-passage to the rear of the building. Before long I saw a glint of light in the hall and went to the front door, which Holmes held open for me.

Here the smell was intense and there were dreadful signs of the Count's recent presence. There were six boxes one of which was open and smelled particularly foul. There was a basin and jug on a filthy old wash-stand. Dirty water remained in the basin, its greyish colour stained as if by blood.

Holmes sighed but recovered soon enough.

"We know there were fifty boxes and we have accounted for them all. Tomorrow will be our day to take a trick or two ..."

A quick search by torch-light revealed nothing else of significance and we left for the Westenra house, our anxiety for Mina unspoken.

CHAPTER SIXTEEN

Although Mina put on a display of liveliness at supper it was noticeable that she ate little. Janos appeared to be watching her anxiously. She had been quiet most of the day and at one point was not to be found until one of the servants saw her sitting in the graveyard on the seat where she and Lucy used to sit. All this came out in supposedly casual conversation but it was clear that Janos, like ourselves, had been disturbed by her behaviour of the morning. Sandor had brought his bags for a prolonged stay and his batman had been accommodated in the servants' quarters. The young soldier said little except the obligatory pleasantries but it was clear that he too was uneasy.

Holmes suggested that I invite Mina to join us for an evening stroll in the garden. It was a clear, moonlit night and quite warm. I saw her frown reluctance but she recovered politely and said she would get her shawl. Holmes and I stood on the lawn, he lighting his clay and I a small cigar. We both noticed her flitting about in the room above, throwing an anxious glance at the tranquil scene. Sandor had dragged Janos into a game of chess, evidently aware of our intentions.

Mina came out, drawing the shawl around her as though feeling chill.

"Ah, there you are," said Holmes, "your uncle is right, a breath of air last thing is always good for one."

"Yes," replied Mina, "but that is not why you, Mr Holmes, suggested this little outing."

"Oh?" he replied mildly, "and what makes you say that?"

"I, I felt very strange this morning," she said quietly, "and I think you both know I did."

"Well, my dear," I said, "you did seem a little ... distracted."

"Yes. When you left in the early hours to go to that awful house, Janos came back to bed. He was very upset because he felt he should have gone with you. We talked about it for a while and then I realised that he had fallen asleep, a deep sleep, the way he did when he was having those dreadful nightmares. I lay there for a long time, at least I think it was a long time, and I began to feel a strange presence in the room. The blinds were up. Janos had left them so when he watched you set out, and the trees threw strange shadows on the ceiling. I remember squirming a little at the strange, moving shapes on the ceiling and on the walls, tree-shaped men with branches like long pointed fingers. And then I was standing at the window and I heard you, Uncle John, speaking to me. I don't remember getting out of bed, or of looking for Janos, or anything ..."

"Did you hear the gun-fire from our little rat-shoot or the siren going when poor Renfield met with his – accident?" Holmes asked her.

She shook her head.

"No, I heard nothing and yet ... and yet I knew that poor man was dead and I don't know how I knew ..."

"Have you spoken with Dr Lukacs today," asked Holmes.

"Yes," she replied, "he was passing when I went for my walk."

"Did he tell you?"

"No ... I said I was sorry about poor Mr Renfield and he said it was for the best, that he was dreadfully injured."

"I see," said Holmes. He smiled at her. "Perhaps we should be getting in, it is a little chill."

He and I turned and headed for the house. But Mina stood her ground.

"Mr Holmes," she said.

"Yes?" he replied.

"What 'little rat-shoot'?"

"Oh, Constanza House, it was infested with rats."

"How did Mr Renfield die?"

"It may have been self-inflicted," said Holmes, "but Renfield believed he was attacked."

"I feel," she said, "that since our 'Council of War' as you called it, you have begun to exclude me from what is going on."

"My dear child," Holmes said, "we are in some danger, all of us, perhaps you especially. You can depend upon it that your uncle and I have your best interests at heart."

She smiled, a sad smile, but a smile nonetheless.

"I know," she said, "I really do know."

With that she walked on ahead of us and we watched through the window as she rejoined her husband.

"I am going to ask Brother Tamas to come here," said Holmes. "I think we may have need of him." We went in as Mina and Janos were preparing to retire for the night. Janos had evidently been a poor opponent for Sandor and had resigned the game.

Holmes prepared a note and Sandor instructed his batman to take it to the monastery.

We had decided to keep watch throughout the night but none of us felt like turning in for their spell of rest. Sandor and I played a game or two between patrolling the house and grounds. Holmes seated himself where he could observe the driveway while reading one of his works of reference, this one in a tortuous Latin script. It was some time after midnight when Holmes got up abruptly to go out and receive Brother Tamas.

I noticed that the tall, gaunt young man was carrying his purple velvet sack embroidered with the yellowy golden crucifix. He listened impassively as Holmes related the events of the past twenty-four hours, but his white hands twitched nervously when Holmes told him of Mina's trance-like state.

The monk asked for seclusion that he might pray and we each of us resumed our vigil through the long night until a piercing scream, short and seemingly stifled, rent the air above us. We hurried up the stairs to the room of Mina and Janos. The door appeared to be locked. Holmes and I threw our weight against it and it barely moved. Sandor added his weight and eventually the door broke from its hinges. We were met with the most appalling, the most terrifying sight imaginable. I felt the hair rise like bristles on the back of my neck and my heart froze.

The moonlight was so bright that through the yellow blind the room was light enough to see. On the bed lay Janos his face flushed, breathing heavily as though in a stupor. Kneeling on the near edge facing outwards was the white-clad figure of Mina.

By her side stood a tall, thin man, clad in black. His face was turned from us, but the instant we saw it we all knew it was the Count.

With his left hand he held both of Mina's hands, keeping them away with her arms at full tension; His right hand gripped her by the back of the neck, forcing her face down on his bosom. Her white nightdress was smeared with blood and a thin stream from an open gash ran down the man's bare breast, which was shown by his torn open garb. As we burst into the room, the Count turned and a hellish look seemed to leap into his face. His eyes flamed red with devilish intent; the great nostrils of the white aquiline nose opened wide and the sharp teeth, behind the full lips of the blood-dripping mouth, champed together like those of a wild beast.

With a wrench which threw Mina back upon the bed as though hurled from a height, he turned and sprang at us.

At the same instant Brother Tamas stepped forward raising up The Host. The Count stopped and seemed to cower for a moment but it was a foul trick to get Janos within his reach. He snatched him up like a rag doll, limp and unconscious as he was.

"Move and I will dash his brains out as I did the maniac." He looked down on Mina, sobbing hysterically and trying to rub off the despoiling bloodstains and the awful smears on her white face.

"You, woman, would you play your brains against mine. You would help these men to hunt me and frustrate me and my designs. It was an ill day for you when you set them upon me! You know now, and they know in part already, and will know more

198

before long, what it is to cross my path. Whilst they played their wits against me – against me who commanded nations – I was countermining them. And you, their best beloved one, are now to me flesh of my flesh; blood of my blood; kin of my kin; my bountiful wine-press for a while and shall later be my companion. You shall be avenged in turn; for not one of them but shall minister to your needs. But as yet you are to be punished for what you have done. You have aided in thwarting me, now you shall come to my call. When my brain says 'come' to you, you shall cross land or water to do my bidding."

He fell silent, sneering at us. We stood transfixed as in a tableaux. Somewhere in the distance there was the sound of the cock's crow.

The Count hurled the helpless body of Janos at us and in that same moment he rushed passed us out of the room. Janos stirred at our feet, moaning as he recovered consciousness. Holmes moved swiftly to the window, running up the blind and raising the sash.

"He is making for the graveyard and the city beyond! He knows the chapel is too dangerous for him now. But he cannot reach his other bolt-holes before day-light. He is on the run in human form! Dangerous, yes, but not more than any other vile murderer."

Janos shook himself and clambered to his feet.

"What ... what happened?" he murmured as he took in the awful scene. Mina screamed, a scream so wild, so piercing, so despairing it will ring in my ears to my dying day. For a few seconds she lay in her helpless attitude and disarray. Her face was ghastly, with a pallor which was accentuated by the blood which smeared her lips and cheeks and chin; from her throat trickled a thin stream of blood. Her eyes were mad with terror. Then she put before her face her poor crushed hands, which bore on their whiteness the red mark of the Count's terrible grip, and from behind them came a low desolate wail which made the terrible scream seem only the quick expression of an endless grief. Brother Tamas stepped forward and drew the coverlet gently over her body whilst I poured a little water into the bowl to wash away the blood.

"In God's name what does this mean?" Janos cried out. "What has happened to my poor darling?"

"The Count!" said Holmes "He held you in a trance while he attacked poor Mina."

"Oh, no, no!" Janos cried in anguish. "God help us, no!"

He rushed to Mina, taking her in his arms. They embraced fervently. When they parted for a moment Mina saw the blood staining his night attire.

"Unclean! Unclean!" she cried. "I must not touch you or kiss you! Oh, God, that I who loves you should be a most dreadful danger to you!"

"No, no!" cried Janos. "It is not too late. Nothing shall come between us."

He embraced her again and she stroked his hair gently as if calming a distraught child. She looked up at Brother Tamas:

"In God's name Father," she said. "Help us, help us."

The Monk stepped forward holding The Host and began to administer a blessing but the instant the wafer touched her forehead she screamed and drew back. It had seared her skin, burning into the flesh like a piece of white-hot metal. Horrified she looked in the mirror and saw as we did the vivid red sliver of a scar that marked her forehead.

"Even the Almighty shuns my polluted flesh!" She pulled her beautiful hair over her face like the leper of old with his mantle. She sank down into an agony of grief as Brother Tamas spoke to her:

"God knows you are innocent, my child. Trust in Him and He will save you."

Janos leapt to his feet:

"No! I will save her! We will save her! We will destroy him before he can take Mina from us! Mr Holmes! Mr Holmes! Tell me that we can destroy him!"

"We know his hiding places," Holmes replied, sympathy mixing with intent. He turned to Brother Tamas.

"As we saw with poor Lucy, fragments of The Host repelled her from her resting place."

Brother Tamas nodded solemnly.

"Then we must act at once," said Holmes. "We have the advantage but it must be pressed home with all speed."

CHAPTER SEVENTEEN

Once more we prevailed upon Janos to stay with Mina. It was pitiful to leave them in their agony but it was surely for the best. We entered Constanza House without difficulty. We left the door open wide to help dispel the foul air and went about flinging open windows to let more light and air into the place.

Sandor wore his sword and used it to slash some of the rotted drapes which fell in clouds of dust as we progressed toward the chapel. Here at least the dirty stained-glass windows afforded some light, though of an eerie kind as motes of dust glistened in the sun's rays.

Holmes had brought screw drivers and wrenches and we set about opening the twenty nine boxes. Brother Tamas watched in silence. It was his first encounter with this part of the Count's machinations. One by one he placed fragments of The Host upon the earth, its pure whiteness standing out on the dark earth.

A coach had been summoned and awaited us at the gates of Constanza House to take us to our next destination, the town house in the Leopold District. Here we broke in as before but this time had the added benefit of being accompanied by a monk as well as an officer of the Hussars.

The place smelled as foul as before, fouler even as we approached the cellar. We were about to descend when we heard the creaking hinges of the front door. We waited with baited breath. For several seconds there was silence. The room we were in was at the rear of the house and it seemed that the intruder might have gone into another direction but no, with an awful suddenness the Count sprung into the room. At that Holmes, in one swift movement reached for Sandor's sword, removing it from the scabbard and lunging at the Count.

His speed was barely thwarted by the diabolical quickness of the Count's leap back. A second less and the trenchant blade would have shorn through to his heart. As it was, the point ripped into the cloth of his coat, making a wide rent from which bundles of bank-notes and a stream of gold fell to the floor. In the next instant the Count dived under Holmes's arm, grabbing a handful of the money, and leaping through the tall window, shattering glass and frame alike as he landed on the gravel below.

We rushed to the window as he turned and looked up at us, his expression an awful mixture of hate and baffled malignity.

"You think to frustrate me!" he cried. "You with your pale faces all in a row, like sheep for the slaughter. You think to deprive me of a place to rest but I have more! My revenge is just begun! The woman is mine and through her you and others shall yet be mine – my creatures to do my bidding and be my jackals when I wish to feed!"

With that he leapt from the terrace on to the lawn and ran across to a gate which led to a lane at the rear. Sandor would have made after him but Holmes stayed him.

"No! Quickly! We must do our work here and get on!"

He led the way down into the cellar and we set about uncovering the boxes so that Brother Tamas could distribute the pieces of The Host.

"We have learned something," said Holmes as he worked with us. "Notwithstanding his brave words, he fears us. He fears time and he fears want! Why else should he scramble so desperately for funds!"

We hastened from the building and Holmes bade our driver make the shortest possible time to the nearest of our destinations, the summer house by the river.

"It is a gamble," said Holmes as we set off, "but even he cannot be in two places at once."

Again we forced entry with little ado. We knew we were in a race against time. We flung open the shutters and ripped out the blinds to illuminate the scene. The six boxes were as we had last seen them and we went about our task with steady hands and steady nerves. Sandor kept look-out, sword in hand and Brother Tamas stood ready with The Host.

We sped to our third destination and entered quickly enough. It took but moments to see that we had been outwitted. One of the six boxes had been removed.

"Attend the other boxes, Watson!" said Holmes as he inspected the area from the box had been taken. Sandor sheathed his sword and came to my assistance as we removed box-lids one by one and Brother Tamas set the fragments in place.

Holmes was on hands and knees as his torch flitted over the floor.

"Two men!" he said. "The Count and one other, a labouring man by the tread of his boots." Holmes sighed. "A toss of the coin might have given us a better choice ..."

Holmes left us to our work and went out into the street. He returned a few moments later. "They had a good start," he said, "twenty minutes or more. There is a puddle in the road, almost dried out. A wagon wheel stopped in it a short time ago."

We hastened to the riverside, calling in taverns, chandlers stores and every point of commerce along the bank describing the Count and the box we were looking for. We must have presented an odd sight – two Englishmen accompanied by a monk and a soldier. At least their presence got us a respectful hearing, apart from a few drunks and derelicts beyond recall. No one could help us. The task was daunting with shipping on both sides of the river and stretching for miles. By chance we came upon the carter who had told us of his work at Constanza House. He had not seen the Count since then but told of us a colleague who had had a windfall that afternoon. Someone had bought his horse and wagon and set him up handsomely. Precious time was lost while we sought the man who had bought a bottle and repaired to his billet, a squalid lodging house near the river. The man was in his cups already but was happy to tell us of the stranger, tall, dark, pale and wide eyed, who had hired him to collect a queer looking box and then, impatient with his slowness, had given him a gold piece for his old work horse and wagon.

"Where was he headed?" Holmes asked him anxiously.

The man shook his head, his hand reaching out for the already depleted bottle. "The city, I reckon," the man told him.

Darkness was gathering when we returned to our waiting coach.

"There is no alternative," said Holmes. "We must return to Mina. We must guard her closely from dusk till dawn."

Both Mina and Janos were clearly relieved when we arrived back at the Westenra house. They stood in the drive, their pale faces betraying their anxiety. We had a sort of perfunctory supper together, and this cheered us up somewhat. It was, perhaps, the mere animal heat of food to hungry people for none us had had a proper meal since the day before. But we were all less miserable since Holmes cheered my niece and her husband with a full account of our day's work, especially the thwarting of the Count by taking his funds for our own 'war chest.' Even Brother Tamas managed to overlook the source of the booty.

Sandor's batman was sent into the city to obtain a fresh supply of the garlic flowers which Holmes and Brother Tamas used in preparing the couple's room for their own safety. Since it would be hard to endure another sleepless night a strict roster was prepared so that all should get some sleep.

When, inevitably, the conversation returned to the prospect of seeking out the Count in his last refuge, Janos grew desperate, unable to contain his anger:

"May God give him into my hand just long enough to destroy the earthly life in him," he declared. "If I could send his soul forever and ever to burning Hell I would do it!"

Mina threw up her hands in abject distress:

"Don't say such things," she said, "or you will crush me with fear and horror." She stopped for a moment, lowering her head before she spoke again:

"I know that you must destroy him just as the Un-Dead Lucy was destroyed so that the true Lucy might live in the hereafter. But that was not a work of hate because you pitied for the poor soul. You must pity him though it may not stay your hands from his destruction."

She looked round the room, looking at us each in turn, as we solemnly acknowledged what she was saying.

Brother Tamas spoke quietly:

"You are right, my child. Think what will be in his joy when he too is destroyed in his worser part that his better part may have spiritual immortality."

But the poor, distraught Janos would have vented his rage again had not Holmes restrained him.

Mina shook her head in despair:

"My dear, I have been thinking all this long, long day of it – that, perhaps, some day ... I too may need such pity and that some other like you, with equal cause for anger, may deny it to me! I pray that God may not have heeded your wild words except as the sad cry of a very loving and sorely stricken man."

With that she got up and held out her hand to Janos and led him off to their room. Holmes, with much persuasion, retired before taking watch, but I doubt he slept. I turned in for young Sandor insisted he had the stamina for the first period. When I passed the open door of the study, Brother Tamas was on his knees, praying silently.

The night passed without event. In the morning we were all somewhat subdued, relieved that the night had been peaceful but frustrated by the knowledge that for all our efforts of the day before, the Count had eluded us. We knew that one earth-box remained and that the Count alone knew where it was. If he chose to lie hidden he could baffle us for years

"A being which has survived for centuries," observed Holmes as we took one of our walks, "can afford to wait and go slow. *Festina lente* may well be his motto. Had we not have crossed his path he would be yet – and indeed may yet be if we fail – the father of a new order of beings whose road must lead through Death, not Life."

"Mina and Janos must come away with us," I said. "It would be better if they put all this behind them."

Holmes paused to re-kindle his pipe.

"It saddens me to remind you of Dracula's words ... 'You shall come to my call. When my brain says 'come' to you, you shall cross land or water to do my bidding.'"

I sighed helplessly. We had reached the iron gate which led down into the graveyard. Holmes pointed silently to the sad figure of Mina, head bowed, on the seat overlooking the city with Janos standing close by.

At least we were doing something. Holmes had been in early conference with Sandor and had got the young officer to recruit some off-duty soldiers to scour the city in a search for the horse and wagon in the hope that it would give us a starting point for another search.

It was late afternoon before we received the news that the wagon had been found in a disused lumber yard. Just before dusk we heard that a horse had been found floating in the river and that the drunken carter, still drinking his bounty, had acknowledged that the worn and sodden bridle had, indeed been his.

Supper was, once more, devoted to our task. Sandor's men were deployed in taverns and on the streets for any sign of the tall dark man. Holmes had spent hours re-reading the histories of the Draculas.

"He was in life a most remarkable man," Holmes told us. "Soldier, statesman and alchemist, which was the highest form of scientific knowledge at that time. He had a formidable brain, learning beyond compare and a heart that knew no fear or remorse. There was no branch of knowledge of his time that he did not essay. Though his brain power may have survived physical death some faculties of his mind are like those of a child. He should have dispersed of those boxes further afield if, as he claims, he was countermining us but he was not quick enough. That is something that we can be thankful for."

Sandor took the first watch and Holmes the second. He roused me in time to have a cold wash before I took over from him. Brother Tamas was getting some much needed rest, the servants were long abed and all was still. I was patrolling the grounds in the fresh night air when I saw the flicker of a lamp in the bedroom of Mina and Janos. I hurried up there without delay.

Mina met me in the corridor. She was pale but composed:

"Uncle John," she said, "I must speak with Mr Holmes."

"Why, my child?" I asked. "What is wrong?"

"I think I can be of help," she said.

A door opened across the hall. Holmes was coming out drawing his robe around him.

"What is it, Mina?" he asked her.

I noticed he had not even been to bed, his energies seeming to build when others wilt from sheer fatigue.

"Mr Holmes, I have heard you speak of hypnotism and thought transference. I know you have studied them. Can you hypnotise me?"

Holmes looked at her for a moment before he spoke:

"Yes I could."

"Then you must do so before the dawn!" she said.

"Very well," he answered. "But we must be quick, dawn is not far off."

We hurried into the morning room. Holmes moved swiftly, preparing a chair for her and motioning her to sit. Without further words he commenced to make passes in front of her, from over the top of head downward, with each hand in turn. Mina gazed at him fixedly for a few minutes, during which my own heart beat like a trip hammer, for I felt that some crisis was at hand. Gradually her eyes closed, and she sat stock still; only by the gentle heaving of her bosom could one know that she was still alive. Holmes made a few more passes and then stopped. I could see that his forehead was beaded with perspiration.

Mina opened her eyes; but she did not seem the same young woman. There was a faraway look in her eyes and her voice had a sad dreaminess in it.

"Where are you?" Holmes asked in a quiet steady voice.

"I do not know," she answered in a neutral way. "Sleep has no place it can call its own."

At this moment Janos slipped into the room but I motioned him to silence. Mina did not stir, her eyes unseeing. For several minutes there was silence. Mina sat rigid and Holmes stood staring at her fixedly. The room was growing brighter. Without taking his eyes from Mina's face he indicated to me to pull up the blind. I did so, and the day seemed just upon us. A red streak shot up and a rosy light seemed to diffuse itself through the room. On the instant Holmes spoke again:

"Where are you now?"

The answer came dreamily, but with intention; it was as though she were interpreting something:

"I do not know. It is all strange to me!"

"What do you see?"

"I can see nothing. It is all dark."

"What do you hear?" I could detect the strain in my colleague's voice.

"The lapping of water. It is gurgling by, and little waves leap. I can hear them on the outside."

"Then you are on a ship?"

"Oh, yes!"

"What else do you hear?"

"The sound of men overhead."

"How many men?"

"Not many. Perhaps one or two."

"Do they speak?"

"No, but I hear them tramp about overhead."

"What are you doing?"

"I am still – oh, so still. It is like Death!"

By this time the sun had risen and we were in the full light of day. Holmes put his hands on Mina's shoulders and guided her head back on the cushion behind her. She lay like a sleeping child for a few moments, and then, with a long sigh, awoke in wonder to see us around her.

"Have I been talking in my sleep?" was all she said.

She seemed, however, to know the situation without telling: she was eager to know what she had said. Holmes repeated the conversation.

"Then he is aboard ship," she said.

"A ship or, more likely, a barge," said Holmes. "God be thanked that we have a clue but I fear he has a good start on us. We know now what was in his crazed brain when he was so desperate for the money that fell from his pockets. Escape! We had him on the run! But if he got passage that very night he has a good start on us."

"I thank God that he has left us," said Mina. "Must we seek him out?"

Holmes looked at her with the utmost sympathy:

"My dear, dear Mina," he said, "now more than ever must we find him even if we have to follow him to the jaws of Hell." She grew pale and nodded helplessly. Holmes went on:

"I would give anything to spare you," he said, "but time is now to be dreaded since he put that mark upon your throat." She ran into Janos's arms, sobbing quietly. He led her back to their room where she rested late into the day.

When the others joined us Holmes told them the news of Mina's trance.

"He is on the way back to Transylvania," he told them. "Of this I am certain. It is a daunting thought for those of us who have been to Castle Dracula but that is where we must go if we cannot waylay him before hand. He is finite. We can destroy him. He has fearful powers but we are all strong in our purpose and stronger still banded together."

Sandor was keen to get after him and would have left that instant but we had to prepare. I, for my part, dreaded the thought of our return to that dreadful place. Sandor made arrangements for his volunteers to canvas the wharves to see if they could find the name of a barge that may have left the night before last though he was not hopeful on such a busy part of the great river.

Meanwhile we had to plan our journey. Holmes deduced that the Count had gone by water, as he had come, because of the greater risks overland.

"The octroi, the toll-keepers, police and the gates of towns and cities and he must fear discovery when he is in a state of helplessness confined between dawn and sunset in his wooden box.

"Rail," he went on "would be just as hazardous with no one in charge of the box. It might be delayed and delay might be fatal with enemies on his trail. It must be water but which route, there are many tributaries of the Danube which can lead to Transylvania." Sandor obtained extensive maps and Holmes and I studied them at length.

"This time we may succeed," Holmes remarked in an encouraging tone. "Our enemy is at his most helpless. If we can come upon him by day, on the water, our task will be over. He has a start on us be he is powerless to hasten. He dare not leave his box lest those who carry him see and throw him overboard where he would perish."

"It seems to me," I said, "the best route from his point of view is the Sereth which joints the Bistritza at Fundu and runs up around the Borgo Pass."

"True," said Holmes, "the loop makes it manifestly as close to Castle Dracula as can be got by water, but the Pruth is more easily navigated. Look, here and here," he pointed to the map, "these symbols indicate rapids of some sort. Without local knowledge they cannot be assessed."

Janos and Sandor sat with us during our discussions. It was decided that we should leave next day for Klausenburg and then would split up so as to make a two-pronged attempt to waylay the Count. Janos was increasingly dubious:

"He must know that we may follow him to the Castle. If it is true that he fought many battles in the region he may have other refuges there."

"True," mused Holmes, "but the histories say that when he was beaten back against greater odds time and again he left the field where his troops were being slaughtered and returned alone to the Castle because he believed that he would, ultimately, triumph.

"On a lesser plane, let us consider the man, the beast he has become. He commits crimes against humanity. He is a criminal. There is a peculiarity in criminals. It is so constant, in all countries and at all times, that even the police who have no time for philosophy come to know it as empiric, that it is. The criminal, the true criminal, always works at one crime. He may be clever, cunning and resourceful but his brain does not have the full stature of manhood, it is in some ways childlike. The Count is a criminal and of criminal type. Nordau and Lombroso would classify him so; and qua criminal he has an imperfectly formed mind. Thus in difficulty he seeks the resource of habit."

Holmes looked at me with a quick smile:

"Heaven knows, he gave Watson and I clue enough that awful night we arrived at Castle Dracula. He told us how he went back from the battlefield where he was beaten, prepared himself with fresh troops and returned to the field and won a great victory. We, in our small way, have driven him from the field ... for the moment."

CHAPTER EIGHTEEN

Shortly before sunset Mina asked to speak with us all. We intended to make the usual preparations for the night against the possibility that the Count might be playing a trick upon us. We were packed and ready to leave in the morning by the one train of the day. Sandor had acquired rifles and ammunition to add to our side arms. Janos and he would be leaving us at Klausenburg. They would hire a fast boat and purchase horses for their part of the pursuit. Holmes and I, together with Brother Tamas and Mina, would travel overland.

I think none of us were surprised by her request. It was becoming noticeable that sunset and sunrise were to her times of peculiar freedom, when her old self could manifest itself without any controlling force subduing or restraining her, or inciting her to action. This mood would begin some half an hour before actual sunrise or sunset and last till either the sun was high or whilst the clouds are still aglow with the rays streaming above the horizon. At first there was a sort of negative condition, as if some tie were loosened, and then the absolute freedom quickly followed. When the freedom ceased the changeback or relapse came quickly, preceded only by a spell of warning silence.

At first, when we were met, she was somewhat constrained and bore all the signs of an internal struggle. After a few minutes she seemed to regain complete control. She motioned Janos to sit beside her on the sofa and asked us to bring up chairs.

"We are all here in freedom," she began, "perhaps for the last time."

Janos began to protest but she soothed him quickly:

"I know, dear; I know that you will all be with me to the end. But in the morning when we set off on our journey, God alone knows what may be in store for us. You must remember, all of you, that I am no longer as you are. There is a poison in my blood, in my soul, which may destroy me; which must destroy me unless some relief comes to us. I know that there is one way out for me, which you must not and I must not take. That I may die now, either by my own hand or that of another before the greater evil is entirely wrought. I know, and you know, that once I were dead you could and would set free my immortal spirit as you did for poor Lucy's. If death, or the fear of death, were the only thing that stood in the way, I would not shrink to die here now amidst you who love me. But death is not all. I cannot believe that to die in such a case, when there is hope before us and a better task to be done, is God's will. Therefore, I on my part give up the certainty of eternal rest, and go out into the dark where may be the blackest things that the world or the netherworld holds!"

We were all silent for we knew instinctively that this was only a prelude.

"You are all prepared to give your lives because they belong to God and you can give them back to Him; but what will you give me?" She paused again but we remained silent:

"I shall tell you plainly what I want for there must be no doubt in this connection between us now. You must promise me, one and all, that, should the time come, you will kill me."

Brother Tamas crossed himself and Janos and Sandor followed him.

Holmes spoke firmly but with due sympathy:

"When would that time be?"

"I think you know well enough, Mr Holmes, but it is my duty to say it – when you should become convinced that I am so changed that it is better that I should die that I might live. When I am thus dead in the flesh, then you will, without a moment's delay drive a stake through me and cut off my head and do whatever else may be wanting to give me rest!"

Brother Tamas fell to his knees praying but the rest of us nodded our agreement despite our pain until it came to Janos's turn:

"Must I, your husband –" he began.

"You must not shrink from it," Mina told him. "You are nearest and dearest and all the world to me but you must promise."

The young man, grey with anguish, nodded helplessly and knelt at her feet, burying his face in her skirts.

"One last word," she said quietly, "and that a warning, a warning which you must never forget: this time, if it comes, may come quickly and unexpectedly and in such case you must lose no time in using your opportunity. At such a time I myself might be – nay! if the time comes, shall be – leagued with your enemy against you."

Much as we might have denied it, that thought remained with us through the final vigil at Westenra House. Holmes took the last watch so as to be ready to hypnotise Mina again if she were willing. I had taken the early watch so as to be up in good time and it was I who looked in on my niece and her husband. She lay there in the moonlight staring at the ceiling. Without a word she got up and came to me, not wishing to disturb Janos. I held open the door and she passed me with the briefest of smiles and went downstairs. Holmes was ready for her and she sat as before. It seemed to take an eternity before she closed her eyes and Holmes began to question her:

"Where are you?"

"I do not know."

"What do you see?"

"It is dark. I see nothing."

"What do you hear?"

There was a long silence before she spoke:

"Water. The lapping of water."

"What else do you hear?"

Again a silence:

"Water," she said again, "the lapping of the water."

"The men on deck? Do you not hear the men?"

"Water," she repeated, "the lapping of the water."

Holmes smiled wearily and eased her head back onto the cushion. I raised the blind but already the rays of the morning sun had slipped into the room. Mina sighed a great sigh and opened her eyes:

"Did I speak to you?" she asked softly. Holmes nodded his head.

"What did I say?"

Holmes crossed to the window, his back to us, looking at the new dawn:

"That the journey continues," he told her.

Mina stretched and found a smile for me:

"Good morning, Uncle John."

"Good morning, Mina," I replied.

She got up and went across the room to the door. When she had opened it, she stopped and turned to us:

"I think it would be for the best," she said quietly, "if you exclude me from knowledge of any plans you make."

Holmes turned, a strange expression on his face, a frown which developed into a thin smile:

"Well said, Mina. Well said."

She nodded and left the room, silently closing the door behind her.

"This is heartbreaking," I said. "To think that we cannot trust this innocent girl."

Holmes began to fill his pipe:

"With the sad experience of dear Lucy, we have no alternative but to heed her warning. We must be thankful she still has the ability to think for herself at least some of the time. My fear is this. If it be that she can, by hypnotism, tell what the Count sees and hears, is it not also possible that he can reverse the process and make her disclose our plans?"

"But she has not been present when we discussed details of the journey or our intention to separate at Klausenburg," I said with some heat.

"That is so," Holmes replied reassuringly, "and is, perhaps more by design than accident. She is a remarkable young woman with more tenacity than poor Lucy who was, sadly, more susceptible to the Count's chicanery."

"You really think so?" I asked with a sense of relief.

"I do," he replied, "but I suggest you caution Janos. It is not a pleasant thing to say but after all the horrors he has endured I am sure he will understand."

I did not relish the task and was relieved when Janos told me that Mina had already extracted the same promise from him.

Shortly before we were due to leave for the station, Holmes raised one final issue that had been at the back of all our minds:

"We have never discussed the possibility of leaving Mina behind – perhaps in the care of the nuns – I am sure Brother Tamas could arrange such an accommodation."

Brother Tamas considered his reply:

"I could and I have thought long on it and prayed for guidance."

Holmes gave him a courteous bow before he resumed:

"I have to say that I do sense gradual change in her. The long periods of sleep during the day, the loss of appetite, the lassitude. I know they have not escaped my friend Watson's notice ..."

I could only nod sadly in agreement. Janos protested, anguish mixed with desperate optimism:

"But when she sleeps she seems tranquil and there are spells of warmth and affection when she wakens."

"She is fighting bravely," Holmes told him, "despite the power of her adversary – our adversary – which is formidable. We do have a solemn compact with her. To leave her in the care of the holy sisters might, on the one hand, advance our campaign, but it would not ensure her safety. I, for my part, believe she should be with us. What do you say, my comrades in arms?"

We all agreed and Janos was clearly thankful.

At that moment Mina entered the room. She looked around, the faint light of a smile in her eyes:

"It is best that I accompany you," she said, as if she had been present at our deliberations. "I know that when the Count wills me, I must go. I know that if he tells me to come in secret, I must come by wile, by any device, to hoodwink even my husband. But I should be with you. I can still be of service since you can hypnotise me even if I may not know what I tell you."

We boarded the train with heavy hearts. We managed to secure two adjacent compartments and passed the long hours quietly, Brother Tamas with his rosary; Holmes with one of his copious volumes; Sandor and I playing piquet; and Mina sleeping in Janos's arms.

We spent the night at the Hotel Royal and dined in a private room. It seemed strange to be retracting our steps and with such an awesome purpose.

Next morning when I opened the door to their room Mina was awake, lying quite still, her eyes wide open and unblinking. She got up as if in a trance and I led the way to our sitting room. Janos had been awake and had watched impassively.

The hypnotic session went as before but for one small addition. When Holmes asked "What do you hear?" she replied, after seconds of silence:

"I hear water, the lapping of water, and, and the lowing of cattle, the tinkle of a bell ..."

When my friend brought her round she asked, as before,

"Did I speak?"

When Holmes replied "Yes," she did not ask further, but smiled distantly and returned to her room. I followed to make sure that she returned safely. When she was about to open the door she hesitated and said:

"He has gone? Janos has gone?"

"Yes," I said gently, "we thought it for the best."

"It is," she said. She smiled at me:

"Thank you, Uncle John."

I kissed her on the cheek but my blood ran cold when I sensed a slight revulsion from her. We parted without comment. Holmes stood at the window as I had left him.

He spoke without turning:

"We are losing her, Watson."

"Yes," I said, "I fear you are right."

He raised an arm to wave silently to someone below. I joined him to see Sandor and Janos being driven out of the courtyard. Sandor gave a cheering salute but Janos was staring ahead.

At Bistritz we found it impossible to engage a coachman willingly to take us to our destination despite the imprecations of Brother Tamas and the local priest. Holmes and I were remembered and regarded with fear as if we had risen from the dead. Finally, after a good deal of money had changed hands, we purchased horses and conveyance outright. Once more we stayed at the Golden Krone but only after the insistence of the aged priest who seemed anxious not to know too much of our purpose. He was clearly as much imbued with the folklore as with his holier beliefs. Brother Tamas remained impassive though he closely observed the silent Mina. Three adjoining rooms were arranged with Brother Tamas on one side, Mina in the centre, and Holmes and I sharing, with a creaking single bed and a chaise, Holmes insisting that I should have the bed.

We slept little and were ready when Mina, unbidden, entered our room just before dawn. When she was sitting trance-like we both observed her for some moments. There was a hardness about the eyes, a hint of deviousness that I had certainly not seen before. Holmes looked at me, running his tongue under his teeth. I nodded agreement with the utmost reluctance, her upper teeth seemed to be sharpening. The signs were slight, almost imperceptible, but they were there. The marks on her throat remained unchanged, tiny pin-pricks, but again, unless it was a trick of the light, the scar on her forehead seemed to stand out with livid clarity.

"What do you see?" Holmes began.

"I see nothing," she responded.

"Are you in darkness?"

"Yes."

"What do you hear?"

"I hear nothing ..."

"What do you hear?" he repeated quietly.

"I hear ... nothing," she replied.

"What do you hear?" he asked again but loudly, insistently.

"I hear ... the water runs fast ..."

"The water runs fast ... What else do you hear?"

"The water runs fast ... the men strain at their oars ..."

"Yes," he said. "They strain at their oars?"

He waited in silence.

Suddenly she spoke again:

"I hear nothing ..." she said in tired whisper "I hear nothing ..."

I had been so engrossed that I had not realised that the sun was up and the room was already bathed in the morning light.

"I would like to sleep now," Mina said.

"You shall later," Holmes told her, "but we must leave directly."

She nodded and returned to her room. Holmes and I went down to the stables where our horses were being harnessed to the coach we had acquired. Brother Tamas was already there. Holmes had prepared a long message for Sandor and Janos to be sent by telegraph and await them at Fundu.

"If it is not a trick," he said, "his route is indeed the Bistritza. They are working their way against the current. If we are wrong we are sending our friends on a wild goose chase ..."

With that he passed the message over the counter and the clerk solemnly counted and recounted the words.

It must have been a strange sight to behold as we set off on our journey with the tall, gaunt monk, the thick cowl on his head, reins and the long whip in his hand, driving us out of the town. The onlookers crossed themselves but, perhaps in deference to Brother Tamas, did not put up the sign against the evil eye.

The coach and its trappings were old but stout enough for the purpose and the horses, a matched pair, were up to their task. The fresh breeze brought some colour to Mina's cheeks but she sat silent for long periods of time, occasionally offering a smile. More disconcerting were the moments when one sensed her staring at us with that hardness about the eyes, a horrid look which I dreaded to see.

Shortly before dark we came upon a small farm where Brother Tamas was able to persuade the farmer and his wife to give us food and shelter.

At dawn Holmes once more hypnotised Mina. But she would only speak of silence and darkness. Either the Count had secured a resting place on land or in some way he was shutting her out.

"I think it is the latter," said Holmes. "I think he knows now he was unwise to tell us of his powers over her. But if he has shut himself off from her, he may not know of our progress, certainly not of our gallant young cohorts."

We reached the Borgo Pass in mid-afternoon. The clouds hung low and foreboding. Holmes was sitting alongside Brother Tamas on the look-out for the turning but it was Mina who found it:

"That is the way," she said. I was startled to hear her speak for she had been silent for a long time.

Holmes turned:

"Are you sure?"

"Yes," she said. "It is the way ... Janos told me."

Holmes whispered something to Brother Tamas and he took the rough path she had indicated.

Mina did not speak again but sat in her trance-like state, rocking and swaying with the movement of the coach. Holmes seemed to have taken on the role of guide and was shrewdly confident as he directed Brother Tamas. Sure enough, after a long journey that would have been monotonous had it not been so pervadingly ominous, we sighted in the gathering gloom the dim outline of Castle Dracula.

Darkness was fast descending. Holmes decided we should make camp while there was still time to gather firewood. Mina remained in the coach while the horses were unhitched and tethered. We had furs aplenty against the cold mountain air and we had bought provisions before leaving Bistritz.

We prepared food but Mina would eat very little. The firelight lit up her pale, drawn countenance and the livid mark on her forehead. As time passed we began to bed down for the night. Holmes took a piece of stick and drew a wide circle around us. Brother Tamas broke up some fragments of The Host and distributed them around the circle. Mina watched this strange ceremony without comment.

I was almost asleep, uncomfortable though I was, when the horses began to scream and tear at their tethers. Holmes and I went over to quiet them. They licked our hands and whinnied low as if comforted and were quiet for a time. Snow began to fall in flying sweeps and with it came a chill mist. The fire was low but even in the dark there was a light of some kind, as there ever is over snow; and it seemed as though the snow-flurries and the wreaths of mist took shape like women in glowing garments. The horses whinnied and cowered as if in terror.

"The women of your nightmare," Holmes murmured to me. It was then that I saw them. They were drawing near the circle, floating in and out of the mist. Holmes stood up to throw a couple of sticks on the fire. The ashes sparked and crackled. He was about to cross the circle for more of our kindling when Mina cried out:

"No! No! Do not go without. Here you are safe!"

He stopped.

"Are we?" he said. "And you? What of you?"

Mina laughed, a laugh low and unreal:

"Me? Why fear for me? No one is safer from them than I." She thrust her hand into her hair and drew it back from her forehead so that the scar shone in the flickering light from the fire.

The wheeling figures of mist and snow came closer, keeping ever without the circle, till – if God had not taken away my reason – they were in actual flesh the same three women who came to me that night at Castle Dracula, the same swaying forms, the hard bright eyes, the same voluptuous lips. As their laughter came through the silence of the night, they twined their arms and pointed to Mina and said in those so sweet tingling tones, like the intolerable singing of water-glasses:

"Come, sister. Come to us. Come! Come!"

Holmes snatched up a flaming branch and Brother Tamas stood by Mina, his crucifix in his hand. My heart leapt with gladness to see the repulsion in her eyes at the horror of these awful women, that told me that she was not yet one of them.

All night they taunted us, disappearing in the swirls of mist and flurries of snow, coming back time after time to call to her; but she remained with us, trembling with fear, yet resolute.

So we remained till the red of dawn began to rise through the snow-gloom, the horrid figures melted in the whirling mist and snow, and the wreaths of transparent gloom moved away toward the Castle and were lost.

I must have slept for a time because the sun was up when Holmes quietly wakened me. Mina was in a deep sleep. Brother Tamas was at his morning prayers. Holmes indicated that we should go toward the Castle. I straightened wearily and rubbed the stiffness out of my bones. As we set off, trudging up the hill toward the Castle, he slung a heavy bag over his shoulder and I thought of the dread task ahead of us. Holmes, puffing on his pipe, made light of his load and might well have been out for a bracing walk on the moors.

We entered the courtyard and made our way to the chapel, that awful place from which we had escaped with poor Janos. Shafts of light broke through the ruins, and the doors sagged as we had left them. The air was oppressive which, for a time, made me feel dizzy.

Holmes moved in and out of the vaults until he found the first of the tombs. He beckoned me to enter the vault and shone his torch on the body of the fair-haired Vampire. She lay in sleep so full of life and voluptuous beauty that I shuddered as though we had come to commit a murder.

I was moved to a yearning for delay which seemed to paralyse my faculties and clog my very soul. But Holmes dropped his heavy load with a clank which brought me back to reality. He opened the bag and took out a stout hammer and a sharpened stave. I held the stave two-handed, with the point over the heart whilst Holmes drove it home. The horrid screeching, the plunging of the writhing form, the lips of bloody foam, were so terrifying that I almost fled. As the body settled into the rigidity of death, Holmes took up a silvery spade and severed the head from the neck.

We found the tombs of her raven-haired sisters and twice more we did the awful deed without exchanging a word. Finally, Holmes drove the spade deep into the earth to cleanse the blade of the foul blood. He placed it and the hammer in the bag, which he slung over his shoulder before leading the way out of the chapel.

We headed back down the hill and walked in silence for some distance before we turned and looked back at the clear line of Castle Dracula in all its grandeur, perched on the summit of a sheer precipice.

Brother Tamas had revived the fire and Mina sat by it, wrapped in furs. The horses stomped nervously as they picked up the cries of distant wolves.

After a warming brew of tea and a few mouthfuls of a rough salami and some bread we began to look for a spot where we could overlook the winding river far below. Brother Tamas put the horses back in harness and walking alongside them as the coach creaked and strained over the rough terrain. Mina sat in the coach, looked pinched and chill despite the swathe of furs. Holmes and I walked ahead and eventually found a commanding spot with a good sight of a loop in the river below and the Castle above. We made camp there, taking turns to watch the approaches below. Brother Tamas made a protective arc for Mina with fragments of The Host and she sat patient but unspeaking. The howling of wolves continued, subsiding for a time and starting up again, sometimes sounding a good deal nearer. We had our rifles supplied by Sandor before the start of the journey, and I prepared them carefully, handing one to Brother Tamas.

As the day wore on a light snow began to fall until in the late afternoon the flurries thickened and the wind got up. Visibility was deteriorating when Holmes cried out:

"Hulloa! There is movement below!"

He lifted up his field-glasses and I scrambled up alongside him as he reported what he saw:

"Mounted men, half a dozen or more! And a lieter-waggon drawn by two pairs."

He lowered the field-glasses and turned to look back at the sun setting beyond the Castle. He took up the glasses again and swept the view below:

"They are racing for the sunset. By Heavens it will be a close run thing! Ahah! I think I see our chaps in close pursuit."

"Do you see the box?" I shouted against the driving wind and snow.

"Aye," he called, "it is lashed to the wagon! Come on, Watson, they must pass below."

With our rifles slung, we hurried down to the rough track. The wolves were howling now, seeming close about us but the flurries of snow made it almost impossible to see. We could hear now the cries of the horsemen and the crack of the whips as they urged on the harnessed pairs.

"They are flogging the horses and galloping as hard as they can," Holmes cried as he unslung his rifle. I followed his example and trained my sights on them, barely visible as they were through the falling snow.

When they were closing on us Holmes fired a couple of warning shots that threw them into confusion, horses rearing and prancing. From beyond them came more shots adding to the melee. The riders cried out in their strange gypsy tongue, the leader evidently trying to rally his panicking band.

We moved forward now, and were able to see Sandor and Janos charge into them, with swords drawn. The Tzgany wielded long knives as they tried to form a ring around the wagon, but we fired into the air to divert them as Sandor leapt from his horse onto the wagon. With quick strokes he cut through the ropes. The wagon stood askew on the uneven ground and it only took a firm shove of his boot to send the wooden box crashing over the side.

The sound of splitting wood rent the air as the lid flew off. Holmes and I ran forward as Janos leapt from his horse and in one single movement drove his sword into the heart of the Count. In that moment I saw the Vampire's red eyes glow with that horrible vindictive look that we had seen before. Holmes snatched a knife from one of the gypsies who was backing away in surrender and cleaved the hideous head from its shoulders. With that the gypsies fled screaming, and as their cries died away one could hear the mournful howling of the wolves, until even that dreadful sound finally diminished.

When we turned breathlessly to look down once more upon the Count's open coffin, we saw that the whole body had crumbled into dust. We became aware that the snow had ceased falling and the last moments of the sun had spread a mellow warmth over the hillsides. There was a silence broken only by the gentle sound of the wind.

Stunned and weary, we made our way to the cleft where Brother Tamas stood guard by Mina. As Janos summed the strength to run toward her, she stood up, her arms opened wide to greet him, a joyous smile upon her lovely face.

"God be thanked," said Brother Tamas. "See! The fallen snow is not more stainless than her forehead! The curse has passed away!"

* * *

In the years that have passed since two elderly gentlemen departed those dreadful slopes and returned to their pipes and slippers and the warm fireside of 221b, Baker Street, London, West, it has been a great delight to me to hear news of Mina and Janos and their little family of three. Holmes, who has never been one to show too great an interest in family affairs, does, nonetheless, ask of them from time to time and always fondly.

Sandor, alas, has not married. His career continues apace, so Mina tells me, and no doubt he is destined for great things but, sadly, there could be but one Lucy in his life. Perhaps for him it is recompense enough to know that he not only avenged his love, but was present at the defeat of a devil and thus secured the happiness of so many young lovers who might otherwise have fallen victim to his evil.

* * *

About the author

Gerry O'Hara began his career as a cub reporter on a provincial newspaper at the age of fourteen. When Michael Powell brought his film unit to town to film scenes for the war-time movie One of Our Aircraft is Missing, Gerry followed them back to London and began a second career which lasted some fifty years.

He was assistant director on films as diverse as Old Mother Riley At Home to Olivier's Richard the Third: from The Loyal Heart, starring Fleet the sheepdog to Preminger's Exodus. From Stryker of The Yard to Tony Richardson's Tom Jones.

In the mid-sixties he made his debut as a screen writer and director of several critically acclaimed (and panned!) movies before moving into television, writing or directing episodes of TV classics like The Avengers and The Professionals.

He wrote the adaptation of the book, Operation Julie, which was aired on three consecutive nights, a first for UK TV, with a nightly audience of thirteen million viewers. He has taught film writing at film schools in London, Sydney and Ljubljana. The British Film Institute have recently released several of his films on DVD, according him cult status for his 1969 movie All the Right Noises starring Tom Bell, Olivia Hussey and Judy Carne. His first film as both writer and director, The Pleasure Girls starring Francesca Annis, Ian McShane and Klaus Kinski has been taught in film schools in the USA.

Sherlock Holmes and the Affair in Transylvania is his first book and foray into yet another new career in his eighties. He has plans for a couple of follow-ups, a Chandler style thriller and a biography.

Find out more about Gerry's writings and his illustrious career at:

www.gerryohara.com

Artwork

The beautiful artwork by PM Rose in this book is available shipped worldwide right to your door as posters, on canvas or in framed prints.

Go to www.gerryohara.com/artwork for more information and to place your orders.

Thanks

This book would simply not have seen the light of day if it wasn't for a few special people.

My boundless gratitude to my wife, Penny, alias P.M.Rose, artist and illustrator; also to my editor and agent Tom Evans, aka The Bookwright, for helping me find yet another career - must be my sixth at least!

At 87, I have to say that I owe endless thanks to former colleagues now toiling at that Great Studio In The Sky. Folk like Sydney Box, a great British producer in his day, always giving breaks to others. Carol Reed, who saw it as his duty to advise and encourage. Otto Heller, a fine cameraman, who got me my big break assisting Laurence Olivier on Richard 111. Otto Preminger for shaking my tree. Anatole Litvak and Vincent Minnelli, who taught me how to live in 'Gay Paree'. Tony Richardson who generously pushed me to the limit and urged me to take up the director's megaphone. He even sent me a director's chair with my name on it ... but on my early 'quickies' there was no time to sit down! Much like this new venture in the world of publishing!

Thanks also to my many former colleagues still on this good planet Earth for their good wishes in this new adventure of mine.

Big thanks to Gerry Hyde for her wonderfully efficient and speedy transcription service and her attention to detail. A high five to Bob Gibson for the eye-catching cover design - books being judged, as they are, by their covers.

Finally, I am eternally grateful to Steve Emecz, my publisher, for his trust, encouragement and, above all, his incredible energy and speed.

Other MX Sherlock Holmes Titles

Short Fiction Collections

The Lost Stories of Sherlock Holmes

Outstanding Mysteries of Sherlock Holmes

Novels

Shadowfall

Barefoot on Baker Street

Rendezvous at The Populaire (vs The Phantom)

I Will Find The Answer (vs Dr. Jekyll)

A Case of Witchcraft

The Sign of Fear, A Study In Crimson (the adventures of the female Sherlock Holmes)

Modern Fiction

No Police Like Holmes

Murder in the Library

The Case of the Grave Accusation

www.mxpublishing.com

Historical / Non Fiction

Close To Holmes

Eliminate the Impossible

The Norwood Author [winner of the 2011 Howlett Literary Award]

A Chronology of Sir Arthur Conan Doyle

Sherlock Holmes, Conan Doyle and Devon

Biographies

Watson's Afghan Adventure

In Search of Dr Watson

Bertram Fletcher Robinson

Special Collections

Baker Street Beat

and many more.........

www.mxpublishing.com